C000121125

FILE COPY
DON NOT REMOVE
PUBLICATION DATE:

January 97

Stranger things

Also by William Paul

Seasons of revenge (Severn House 1985)
Mummy's boy (Macdonald 1987)
The hindmost (Macdonald 1988)
The lion rampant (Macdonald 1989)
Dance of death (Severn House 1991)
Sleeping dogs (Constable 1994)
Sleeping pretty (Constable 1995)
Sleeping partner (Constable 1996)

STRANGER THINGS

William Paul

Constable · London

First published in Great Britain 1997
by Constable & Company Ltd
3 The Lanchesters, 162 Fulham Palace Road
London W6 9ER
Copyright © 1997 by William Paul
The right of William Paul to be
identified as the author of this work
has been asserted by him in accordance
with the Copyright, Designs and Patents Act 1988
ISBN 0 09 476870 6
Set in Linotron Palatino 10 pt by
Pure Tech India Ltd
Printed in Great Britain by
Hartnolls Ltd, Bodmin

A CIP catalogue record for this book is
available from the British Library

1

Monday: 09.34

The fallen angel was embedded in the ground. It looked as if it had flown straight into it by accident, like a lost plane into a hillside. One arm and clenched fist was above the surface, and one eye of the half-hidden face, and the graceful curve of the feathered wings, and the legs tied down by a dozen silvery strands of spiders' webs. All around it in a rough oval the dew-damp grass seemed greener, as though the angel's energy was leaking into the soil and nourishing the unseen roots.

The dead girl lay alongside the angel in a sad parody of its position. She was face down, one arm was outstretched, and the coldness of the night and the stiffening of her dead muscles had suspended her feet a few inches above the ground. The spiders had already been at work. Frost crystals sparkled in the dead girl's long hair and bloomed on her dark quilted anorak and light-blue jeans, mimicking the irregular pattern of lichen patches creeping over the stone skin of the angel.

David Fyfe stepped around the pedestal that had once been the platform on which the angel stood. The disused cemetery was like a secret world, suddenly revealed by archaeologists. There was hardly a grave where the stone had not been split or had not been toppled from its original site. Ivy covered the encircling wall. Rust ate away at the wrought-iron entrance gates that stood permanently open and bound to the ground by clinging weeds. The graveyard was an unkempt mass of a long summer's growth of bracken and nettles and waist-high grass with the memorials to long-forgotten people gradually being submerged as the carved names on the stones were wiped smooth by the relentless passage of time. Overhead, the branches of huge, spreading sycamore trees virtually blocked out the light, making solid shapes of the drifting shadows. The only signs of life among the dead were the birds calling in the trees, small animals scuttling in the undergrowth, and the network of narrow paths worn and hard-packed flat by people walking their dogs. That was how she had been found, by an inquisitive spaniel called Molly who had the sense to ignore all her obedience training until a reluctant owner was obliged to beat a new path through long grass to find out what was wrong.

Fyfe crouched down in the space between the fallen angel and the dead girl, careful not to let the hem of his heavy tweed coat trail in the frozen mud. A familiar black mist of depression settled on him as it always did when he was confronted with a dead body, especially that of a young woman who was only a little younger than his own daughter. Don't take it personally, he told himself. Be professional. Be detached. Don't let it get to you. It never worked.

He could hear the constant rumble of traffic beyond the wall and, somewhere high above, the drone of a light plane heading west across the city to the airport. He sighed deeply and his breath billowed out in a vapour cloud on the frigid air before slowly vanishing. It was either September or October, he couldn't remember if the month had changed over the weekend, but it had been a mild summer well above average for sunshine and below average for rainfall. He supposed the cemetery and its encircling wall at this time in the morning must form some kind of frost hollow.

The day had been tinged with optimism before this call-out. His daughter Kate had phoned the previous night to say she was coming home on a spur-of-the-moment visit that evening. She seldom came north since getting married, even calling off last Christmas and New Year because of pressure of work. He was due to go to London tomorrow on a three-day training course on hostage negotiation but hadn't got round to phoning Kate to tell her he would be dropping by. He probably wouldn't be able to get out of the course and that meant he would only have one night with his daughter, depending on how long she was going to stay. But with an almost still-warm murder victim to look after, there was always the chance that he might not now have to go to London. Whatever, he planned to sneak away

6

around lunchtime and collect Kate from Waverley Station personally.

A body has been found in a graveyard, they had told him as soon as he arrived at the office. Oh really, how unusual, he had replied. They had to go and get Bill Matthewson to persuade Fyfe it was not a joke because Matthewson didn't have a sense of humour and therefore could not be disbelieved. And here she was, the anonymous dead girl, lying with the angels in an abandoned inner-city cemetery. No handbag or purse, or anything in her pockets to show who she was. There were no obvious signs of violence on her and the cause would not be known until after the post-mortem. All the crime scene procedures had been followed and photographs taken. A bureaucratic memorial to the girl would survive to live on in police records whoever she was. She seemed too well dressed to be a long-term junkie or one of the homeless street people. Her training shoes were new and expensive, her anorak very good quality. It could be suicide. It could be natural causes. It could be murder. The only certainty for the present was that it was death.

Fyfe's eyes strayed to the angel's wings. The grey stone was carved into the representation of overlapping feathers. Lines of black dirt marked the grooves. As he looked a tiny, red-breasted robin perched for a couple of seconds on the apex of one wing and then flew away. Following the flight of the bird he noticed for the first time the inscription on the empty plinth. The name was partially obscured by green moss and so worn he could not make out all the letters. Her name began with the letter V or U. He peered more closely and after a couple of attempts read Virginia. The dates below were legible: 1874–1890. The ancient bones of a sixteen-year-old girl who had never grown old were beneath his feet. He imagined the skeleton stirring a little, pushing upwards, disturbing the undergrowth, failing to break through. The bones relaxed, resigned to their imprisonment. Dry earth trickled through eye and nostril holes in the skull. A flash of horrified panic made Fyfe's chest tighten and his heart beat more rapidly. He shivered and had to peer more closely at the fallen statue's plinth to be able to make out the badly weathered quotation: Until The Day Breaks.

Fyfe looked up at the blankness of the grey morning sky through the ragged circle of leaf-heavy branches that marked the perimeter of the small cemetery. Then he turned his attention to the dead body that lay above ground. He hooked a finger under the girl's hair where it fell across her face and lifted it up. The frost had welded the strands of hair together so that it moved as a single unit, a trapdoor that revealed that the girl's left eye was open. In the middle of the ice-blue iris the black, hugely dilated round of the pupil had Fyfe's crouching image caught inside it in miniature.

He snatched his hand away from her face and stood up. He was imagining a beautiful girl reaching out to embrace him. As she touched him and her arms went round his neck she was transformed into a skeleton, the skin falling away from her bones as though she was stepping out of a figure-hugging dress. He shivered again, grunting audibly, and pulled his coat more tightly around him to shut out the suddenly terrible cold.

Weak sunlight was now filtering through the overhanging trees, pouring warmth inside the walls, making thin trails of steam rise from the undergrowth. Fyfe walked away quickly, retracing his footsteps among the gravestones as exactly as possible so as not to disturb any potential evidence at the scene. The shadows moved with him. He glanced back nervously, knowing there was nothing to fear, nothing waiting behind the stones to jump out on him, but fearing it anyway.

He kept looking back until his view of the girl's body was blocked by the fallen angel which seemed to be watching him retreat through a single, sightless eye. He stumbled and put out his hands to save himself, just managing to maintain his balance with an awkward skip and a jump. Yesterday she had been a beautiful young woman with her whole life ahead of her. Today the process of biological corruption was already under way in her lifeless body as it began to decompose. Ashes to ashes, dust to dust and all that. Poor little angel, Fyfe thought. No simple kiss from him would reawaken the sleeping beauty. He dug his hands deep into his pockets and forced himself to smile foolishly as a diversion from the depressing reality. Don't take it personally, he told himself. Life had to go on.

At the cemetery gates the van was waiting to collect the girl and take her to the mortuary for the post-mortem. They were ahead of themselves with their argument about whether they should lower the wheels on the stretcher or just carry it because of the rough ground. The scene of crime unit had a lot to do before they got their hands on the body bag. Four men in white plastic overalls were emerging from another unmarked van. The serious incident caravan was being unloaded from a lorry. A uniformed constable stood guard at the entrance, another pair of uniforms were sitting inside their orange and white car. Matthewson was leaning against the wall, looking uncomfortable while a young woman with long black hair and a long black coat talked at him.

Fyfe ducked under the blue and white tape at the gates and re-entered a world that was neat and ordered and much less sinister. A strip of grass in front of a row of houses was cut short. Young trees were held up by stakes and their slender branches had big leaves hanging from them. He felt more in control. He noticed for the first time an antique cast-iron notice declaring that the graveyard was private property. The biggest tree of all stood guardian just inside the gates, its heavy branches dappling the cold sunshine on the ground around it. The woman in the black coat stood in front of Fyfe and stuck a microphone in his face. Her loose-fitting dress underneath billowed in the breeze and he caught a glimpse of a lacy black bra strap. He remembered that she was a reporter with the local radio station. He had spoken to her before but couldn't remember her name.

'Andrea Brady, Inspector Fyfe,' she said, pleading with her eyes. 'Radio Forth. Can I ask you some questions? I can make the news on the hour if we're quick.'

'Chief Inspector it is, Andrea. What do you want to know?'

'What's going on?'

'Turn that off and I'll tell you.'

He closed his hand over the microphone and waited until she switched off the tape recorder hanging from her shoulder.

'We have a suspicious death.'

'Murder?'

'Don't know yet.'

'Who is it?'

'Unidentified female.'

'Young?'

'A wee bit younger than you, I would say, but not much. That's it. You now know as much as I do. There will probably be more this afternoon.'

'Injuries?'

Fyfe saw the dead girl's apparently unviolated body lying beside the fallen stone angel. Until The Day Breaks was a strange inscription to carve on a gravestone, he thought. For Andrea's benefit he shook his head and stepped to one side to indicate that the interview was over. She understood and turned away. She lifted the bottom of her coat to avoid the wet grass and her dress swirled like a ballroom dancer's, exposing her legs just above the knee. She was already composing her report for the next news bulletin from the few scraps of information he had given her. He heard her mutter his name under her breath.

Beside Fyfe, Matthewson yawned. He had been about to finish his shift and go home to bed when the call came in.

'Cheer up, Bill,' Fyfe said. 'The day has just begun.'

'Sorry.' Matthewson pushed himself away from the wall. 'Is that it then? Have you seen all you need to see?'

'That's it.'

'What do you think?'

'A nice looking girl.'

'Is she one for us?'

'Probably. Young girls don't go to sleep in cemeteries by choice normally.'

The scene of crime squad were ducking under the tape. Matthewson yawned again. 'It will be a few hours before we can move the body out, I suppose?'

Fyfe looked back over his shoulder and from where he stood the cemetery seemed much less cold and threatening. The reality was less sinister, distinctly amusing even. The smile on his face was no longer forced. He couldn't help himself.

'Remember it is a cemetery,' he said. 'Please make sure you take the right body.'

2

Monday: 11.05

The train was speeding down the east coast. On one side the flat grey span of the North Sea licked the horizon like a dead man's tongue, on the other the undulating East Lothian countryside was piebald with moving patches of sunshine and shadow. Bruce Davidson rested his forehead against the window glass and closed his eyes. The rhythm of the vibration penetrated the bone and touched his brain, soothing it a little after its alcohol and drug inflamed excesses. He tried to remember what had happened the night before but his memory was empty except for a fog of constant jungle noises, the screeching of the parakeets and the scuttling of invisible animals. In the morning he had woken with a sense of unspecified panic telling him to get out. So he had run. No time to find the girls, but they were used to his unreliability and would catch up soon enough. He would feel better by then and capable of dealing with them. They knew where to find him. They had been separated before and found each other. It wasn't like them to lose him anyway. Why hadn't they stayed with him? How often had he warned them? Where the hell were they?

A fragment of memory tumbled through his consciousness, too fast for him to make out what it was. He visualized running legs, a pair of hands clasped one over the other to hold something inside, a female shriek like fingernails scratching on glass. Uncertain laughter. Unquiet silence. He chased after the memory but it was far too quick for him, disappearing like a rabbit down a hole. He dived after it but his face ploughed into the ground. Sitting in the train, he realized that he had the heel of his hand pressed against his nose.

It was a long journey to London. He badly needed to get some sleep but knew it was going to be difficult because of the state he was in. It bothered him that he had been unable to find a seat that would allow him to face the direction of travel. He hated

11

travelling backwards but the train was crowded and there was no option. It was a bad omen, like the pigeon at the entrance to the station that had swooped down and almost hit him, a sinister deliberation in its attempt. If he linked it all to not knowing where Ginny was it would begin to worry him. But he didn't want to think like that. He didn't want to think at all.

Davidson opened his eyes. A fat woman with a leather jacket and skull and crossbones earrings was sitting diagonally opposite him. She had tiny features in a large full-moon face and orange and black streaked hair. Her child was in the window seat, equally chubby and not obviously either male or female. It held a bunch of colouring pens in its hand and stared at Davidson curiously, like an artist sizing up a subject before beginning to paint. Its head also had small features in a round expanse of white flesh topped by a shock of dirty blond hair. Davidson watched as the flesh of both mother and child crept over their lips and nostrils and eyes, oozing like spreading candle wax to seal off their faces and make their heads entirely smooth and featureless apart from the hair sprouting up. The old man sitting beside him reading a computer magazine had gone the same way. Davidson laughed and the three turnip heads turned to look at him blankly. He laughed again and pressed his forehead more firmly against the window to check the hallucination. It wouldn't do for him to begin believing that he was travelling inside the gut of a worm boring into a turnip. It wouldn't do at all. Imagining it was all right, believing it was insane. As Ginny was fond of telling him, sometimes it was better to be mad because that way the world made a lot more sense.

'Tickets please. Thank you, madam.'

The inspector was only two seats back now, his gruff voice preceding him, looming louder. Irrational panic leeched through Davidson like sweat through open pores. A northbound train passed on the parallel track and the window whumped inwards, nudging Davidson's head and making his teeth click together sharply. He got up, mumbling an excuse me, and knocked stuff off the table as he slid out from behind it and left the turnip heads. The toilet between the carriages was vacant. He locked the door, dropped his trousers and sat down with his face in his hands. Another multicoloured fragment of memory fluttered above him. He snatched at it but missed and it drifted away.

There was a hammering on the door. A muffled shouting. He looked up as the door slid open and the ticket inspector's face, impossibly small at the top of a pyramid body, peered down at him. The peak of his cap was like a razor blade.

'Do you have a ticket, sir?'

'Of course,' Davidson replied evenly, surprised at the strength of his voice.

He reached up to hand over an envelope from his inside pocket, rocking on the toilet as the train went round a bend. There were people passing behind the ticket inspector, smirking as they pretended not to look.

'Oh, sorry, sir,' the inspector said, deflating from his great height so that his head was bigger than his squashed body and he was almost on eye level with Davidson. 'I'm sorry. I thought there was a problem.'

Davidson waved him away magnanimously, accepting the return of the envelope. 'Just close the door,' he sighed.

'There are three tickets, sir. You have travelling companions?'

Davidson looked round the narrow toilet compartment as if he was expecting to see somebody else there. His hands dangled down to the trousers round his ankles. Why weren't they with him? Where were they? He couldn't remember. No memories came out of the inky smooth blackness inside his head. But there was something there, something terrible lurking. He blinked and felt very afraid.

'Is my face red, Inspector?' he asked in a calm voice.

The inspector frowned and studied him carefully. The tip of his nose seemed to stretch like Pinocchio's until it was right up against Davidson's face.

'No,' he said finally.

'Then wherever they may be, you can rest assured my companions are most definitely not up my arse.'

There was a delayed reaction until understanding dawned, then the ticket inspector jerked back. The door slid shut. Davidson locked it and the light glowed red. In the restored privacy he pulled out a square of tin foil which he unfolded to expose a thin pile of crumbled cannabis resin. From his tobacco tin he took an already prepared roll-up. With extreme care, his tongue poking from the corner of his mouth and swaying with the motion of the

13

train, he used the tin foil as a funnel to pour the blow in the end so that it filtered down into the loose tobacco. He didn't spill a single grain. He twisted the end to hold the contents in and lit it with his gas lighter, sucking hard to fill his lungs. The anticipated rush of euphoria, more psychosomatic than physical, came within ten seconds. It was like free-falling into the sudden calm of deep water.

Davidson inhaled deeply again, now unafraid of whatever lurked in the blackness. The cigarette paper flared. He sat back. The window at his shoulder was opaque with a small circle in the centre through which he could see the sky, at least he supposed it was the sky but it didn't have any distinguishing features. The clear glass was a light-grey smudge in the midst of a darker grey mass.

He realized that he was drowsy, and knew this was unusual because a quick drag normally pepped him up, put some energy into him as though jump leads had been connected to his ear lobes and the ignition fired. Instead, his head sagged. He thought of his brain glowing bright red in a world that was a uniform shade of darker red, and the two reds were merging. Davidson slumped against the window, his head resting on the glass, bouncing to the rhythm of the motion. The half-smoked roll-up slipped from his fingers into the sink and rolled into a small pool of water to be extinguished with a whispered hiss and a tiny curl of vanishing smoke.

3

Monday: 11.16

Fyfe didn't hurry although the phone was ringing in his office. The heat from the rim of the plastic cup of coffee was hurting his fingertips as he reached into his jacket pocket for his keys. He had only one free hand to work awkwardly through the bunch and single out the proper key and slip it into the lock. The door had just enough resistance to cause a little of the scalding liquid to splash out of the coffee cup onto his fingers. He cursed loudly and

14

quickly put the cup down on the desk, spilling some more onto the pieces of paper scattered there, and put his fingers in his mouth. Superintendent Les Cooper had met him on the stairs and informed him, before he had the opportunity to say anything, that Connor Harper was coming in from leave the next day to take the lead in the murder case so that Fyfe didn't have to abandon the hostage negotiating course. If Fyfe just held the fort today that would be fine. And with that Cooper passed on.

Fyfe felt the accusing eye of the fallen statue watch him from the other side of the city. The phone kept ringing steadily. Over and over again. He took a sip of the coffee and grimaced at the chemical bitterness. He snatched up the phone and spoke irritably.

'Fyfe.'

'Hello, stranger.'

The sound of Hilary's voice was instantly recognizable to him, damping down his bad temper in sympathy with the rapid cooling of his burned fingers. He had not seen or heard from Hilary for months. They had met at a party, indulged themselves in a brief flirtation rather than an affair, and then drifted apart again. He remembered the short black dress she had been wearing when he first laid eyes on her, and the tight jeans and loose white tee-shirt of more casual encounters, and the warmth of his hand on the small of her back and the taste of her tongue running over his front teeth. There had been no sex, although it had come close sometimes. Once a couple of weeks had gone past without them seeing each other, Fyfe had presumed that was an end to it. Now he was pleasantly surprised that she should take the initiative and contact him.

'Hilary,' he said. 'Hilary. It's you.'

'It is. I haven't heard from you for ages.'

'Sorry about that. I've been meaning to phone, I've just never had a minute. You know what it can be like.'

'I thought you'd forgotten me.'

'No chance of that.'

'Because I haven't forgotten you. What do you think happened this morning?'

'Don't know.'

'My swimming partner called off from our lunchtime date and I was wondering who I could ask to go with me. Then I heard your name on the radio. It was a sign, don't you think?'

15

'Spooky.'

'So? Do you fancy it then?'

'Fancy what?'

'A lunchtime swim with me?'

Fyfe hesitated. He fancied it greatly, of course, but he couldn't really afford the time, not with the preliminaries of the murder investigation to watch over and Kate to be met off the train and stuff to get ready before he left for London. But he didn't want to put Hilary off. The unexpected prospect of meeting her again had shaken him out of the slough of depression caused by starting the day confronted with the untimely death of a young girl. And he was going south for the rest of the week. There was no way out of that. If he didn't take her up on her invitation, Hilary would think he wasn't interested. He couldn't say no.

'I'd love to,' he said. 'But I don't have a thing to wear.'

'Interesting. Can't you borrow a pair of trunks?'

'That shouldn't be too difficult.'

'I'll meet you at the entrance to the baths then at half past twelve.'

He couldn't say no now. It was settled. He would have to phone Sally and get her to collect Kate from the station. He could tell her he had been held back because of the murder. And he would tell Cooper and the rest that he couldn't get out of the arrangement to collect his daughter at such short notice. What people didn't know, wouldn't hurt them.

He believed there was at least one pair of swimming trunks that would fit him in the tangled pile of towels and socks squashed into the lost property locker in the shower room. If he was lucky, he would manage at least an hour with Hilary. That would definitely put him in a better mood.

4

Monday: 11.40

Sally Fyfe waited at the main exit from platform eleven as the London train drew into Waverley Station, its passengers rising from their seats so that every carriage seemed impossibly full. She stood, bobbing up on tiptoe every few seconds to try and catch a first glimpse of her daughter Kate. All along the platform in both directions other people were acting in a similar fashion. If it wasn't for their different clothes, it could have been an image created by endlessly reflecting mirrors. In front of the platform the long train gradually slowed to a complete halt. The doors sighed open and the passengers began to disembark and mingle with the people already waiting on the platform, adding to the general air of confusion. It had been, Sally had calculated, more than six months since she had last seen Kate, far too long for mother and daughter to be apart. Sally was anxious. She had the feeling that there was something badly wrong. The unexpected phone call, the strained voice, the hasty journey north, almost certainly pointed to marriage problems. It was just over two years since the wedding and Sally had had her suspicions for half that time. Now they would be confirmed. Kate would have learned that all men were bastards. Every one. No exceptions. Dave couldn't make the time to meet her at Waverley. Too busy, he said. Too busy to look after his own daughter.

She saw Kate, one of the last to get off the train, stepping down backwards and pulling a heavy suitcase after her. She recognized her instantly, despite the shapeless coat and the floppy hat hiding her face. Things were bad, Sally thought. Kate was a fashionable dresser. To be seen in public in that state meant she was deeply depressed. And underneath her hat she could see that Kate's hair was lank and greasy.

'Darling,' Sally said as she walked through the rapidly dispersing crowd. 'It's good to have you home.'

'Mother,' Kate replied sheepishly.

They hugged. Kate had a pair of black sunglasses on. Another bad sign. The suitcase trundled behind them on its little wheels as they walked to the car parked in the row of short-term spaces. Sally didn't say anything until it was in the boot and they were belted into the front seats.

'What are you going to tell me, Kate?' Sally asked.

'I don't want to tell you,' Kate said.

'Just tell me.'

'I'm pregnant.'

17

Sally didn't say anything. Any instinct to rejoice was firmly held down by a premonition of imminent misfortune. The sounds of the busy railway station outside swirled round the car. A couple walked past pushing a trolley, behind them a young child eating a chocolate bar stared through the windscreen. Kate was reaching up to remove her sunglasses.

'And I've left him for good. I've walked out. He can rot in hell as far as I am concerned.'

At first, Sally thought it was a joke; remove one pair of glasses and have another pair on beneath. Then she realized that the dark marks encircling her daughter's eyes were bruises. There was a cut on her eyelid that had stitches in it, loose ends sticking out like the shafts of tiny arrows. Purple-coloured swelling ruined the symmetry of her face. One side was hardly touched, the other looked like a boxer's after a hard fight.

A surge of anger that made Sally's face burn with suffused blood was rapidly replaced by a wave of nausea. She didn't say anything. The anger came back, cramping her muscles, making her grind her teeth until her jaws were sore. She leaned across the front of the car to put her arms round her only daughter to hold her close. Kate's forehead bumped painfully against the side of her chin, bringing tears to her eyes. Together, the two women wept at the iniquity of life.

5

Monday: 12.38

The swimming baths on the south side were quaint and old-fashioned with swing-door changing cubicles around the edge of the pool, and an arched glass ceiling supported by exposed rafters. In a burst of renovation fever, the original wood panelling had been painted a garish orange and yellow, the colours reflected in the tee-shirts and shorts of the lifeguards, giving the place the look and feel of a 1950s holiday camp. Hilary shaded her eyes as they emerged from the turnstile straight into the main area. 'I warned you it was tasteful, didn't I?' she said, flapping her hand in front of her face.

They had met outside, she arriving a few minutes after Fyfe, coming up behind him and grabbing him by the waist. She was casually dressed in a pleated skirt and sandals. They kissed, exchanged nice to see you again pleasantries and then stopped and looked at each other. In that pause, a fleeting instant of time, Fyfe was uncomfortably aware of the same sense of foreboding he had experienced when crouched over the dead body of the young girl earlier that morning. He knew he should stay away from Hilary because she was a threat to the stable order of his life which had settled into a smooth flow over the last few months. He had no outstanding problems, no distractions, no temptations. Now here, suddenly, was Hilary again. And it worried him that if the unknown girl in the cemetery had not died and he hadn't answered the radio reporter's simple questions, then Hilary might not have contacted him and the continuing distance between them would have made it more and more unlikely that the connection would ever be re-established. His life would have taken a different course altogether. The events of the morning, he thought while standing on the pavement outside the swimming baths with Hilary beside him, were a defining moment. Something, although he had no idea what, was beginning to happen.

The pool was relatively empty, only a couple of people ploughing up and down a roped-off lane and a group of teenagers splashing with jolly abandon in the shallow end. The trunks Fyfe had commandeered from the locker were long-legged and baggy. They changed in adjacent cubicles and Fyfe was first out. He was in the showers, enjoying the all-enveloping deluge of warm water, when Hilary joined him. She had on a simple one-piece shiny black costume that was like a second skin over her slim body. The time lapse switch turned off the shower and he was left standing, dry-eyed, staring at her unsubtly. She smiled back with every indication that she knew exactly what he was thinking, and that was the effect she intended to have on him. She turned her back, punched the wall switch, and rose up on the balls of her feet to meet the flood of water. She swept her wet hair backwards over the top of her head and presented her face to the full force of the shower. Fyfe took a deep breath, sucking in his stomach, and regretted his pasty white flesh. He lifted his face so that he was temporarily blinded by his own personal downpour.

Hilary took to the designated lane for the thirty lengths of breast stroke she promised to do while Fyfe pottered around aimlessly as he conditioned himself to the lower temperature. He wasn't much of a swimmer, preferring to float with his arms out along the sides of the pool while watching Hilary's head rising and falling in front of the graceful curve of her following body. The pool got busier with lunchtime trade in for a quick dip and out again. The volume of noise increased, echoing up into the roof space. Fyfe found that if he ducked under the surface the quality of the sounds changed significantly, became more distant and soothing, so he started floating on his back with just his ears below water and got a fright when hands pressed against his chest and pushed him under. He came up spluttering to see Hilary grinning cheekily at him.

'Careful,' he said. 'I'm fragile.'

'I would have rescued you.'

'Go on then.'

Fyfe fell back in the water, pushing himself down towards the deep end. Hilary swam round behind him and positioned herself so that he was lying against her and her chin was against the top of his head with her arm over his upper chest and neck. If he closed his eyes he could easily forget all his worries and the nagging sense of guilt that told him he should make some effort to get back to work.

'There now,' Hilary said. 'How does that feel?'

It felt good. Fyfe made an appreciative but unintelligible noise and Hilary's arm tightened across his neck, slightly restricting the air supply but not so much that he needed to complain about it. It felt very good.

'I thought you were busy today, couldn't spare me much time?'

'I am, I can't.'

'Well, I have to go back to work.'

'Uh, so do I. A shame, isn't it?'

'It certainly is but we'd better make a move.'

20

Fyfe repeated his appreciative grunt and reluctantly broke the touch of their bodies. He expected his feet to find the bottom but they had drifted too far and he had to swim to stay afloat. Hilary kept hold of his neck and one of her legs curled round his waist as he swam to the steps at the corner of the pool. Hilary climbed out first and he let his hand trail down her thigh as he pretended to help her. She turned and offered a hand to pull him up.

They showered together, sharing a slippery sachet of shampoo Hilary fetched from her cubicle, not saying anything lest they should be overheard by other swimmers now rushing back to city centre offices. Hilary's skin had a healthy rosy sheen that contrasted sharply with the outline of the black costume. They didn't exchange another word until they were both dressed and standing facing each other on the pavement where they had renewed their relationship an hour earlier.

'Thanks for keeping me company,' she said.

'My pleasure. We must do it again.'

'We must, but you know what I'd like to do again?'

'Give me a clue.'

'Remember how you once came round to visit with a bottle of wine?'

'Yes, I remember.'

She touched his forearm. 'I'd like to do that again.'

Fyfe nodded. 'Sounds good to me.'

There was no chance of mistaking or misinterpreting such an invitation. Soon after they had first met he had gone round to her home and they had drunk wine and lain on the sofa in a similar position to the one they had just untangled themselves from in the swimming pool. Then, she had made it plain beforehand she wasn't going to sleep with him, but this time he got the impression there would be no limiting conditions imposed. He began to calculate when it would be possible. He couldn't go tonight, not with Kate due back and then he had three nights in London. Hilary waited patiently as he explained. Her hand was still on his forearm, pressing urgently.

'We'll make it Friday then.'

It was obvious Hilary wasn't going to let him go without a firm commitment to a specified date. Fyfe could have argued. He could have said he would be immersed again in the body in the cemetery murder case as soon as he got back. But he didn't want to make difficulties because the offer might never be made again. The time was ripe now, leave it too long and it would rot away. The young girl lying face down beside the fallen angel would never know the touch or the love of another person now. The world had a habit of wrecking people's carefully ordered plans for their lives and giving no second chances. Fyfe might find himself face down being measured for a coffin soon enough. He wanted to lie full out against Hilary on that sofa and feel the beating of her heart under her rib cage and the warm hollow of the small of her back under the palm of his hand.

'What about your husband?' he asked, lowering his voice.

'He's left me. He won't be there.'

'I will then.'

'I knew you would.'

The bargain was sealed. Hilary stepped forward and kissed him, her tongue sliding over his front teeth. Fyfe watched her walk away, fascinated by the swing of her skirt and the creases of skin at the back of her knees. A young woman coming out of the swimming pool doors bumped into him, distracting his attention as she dropped her bag and snatched it up again. She mumbled an apology. When Fyfe looked back along the street Hilary had disappeared.

6

Monday: 13.10

The dog was a classic mongrel, assembled over the course of several canine generations from retriever, Labrador, Alsatian, greyhound, poodle, collie, terrier and husky. The result was quite a small dog, one triangular ear permanently sticking up, the other hanging down. Mostly he ran wild on the estate and nobody much bothered him because he had been sterilized as a puppy, giving him a characteristic stiff-legged gait, and was never aggressive or threatening. Local people knew his name was Rex. He wasn't a stray. He belonged to a childless couple who were out working all day and went sailing at the weekend. They kept him in the back garden, occasionally repairing the gaps in the fence as a token gesture at control, but in the main they didn't want to know. Rex returned home each evening to be fed and to lie asleep in front of the hissing gas fire. If there was no one there he had the choice of several garden sheds or sheltered spots, and the next-door neighbour was tolerant enough to give him a place if necessary. His easy life meant that he was a friendly and contented dog but he was still wary of strangers, having suffered the occasional kick or smack over the nose from being too trusting and eager to please.

Which was why Rex sat down at a safe distance and cocked his head to one side to look at the strange woman sitting with her back against the wall and her legs splayed out in front of her. With the children at school, he was surprised to find anybody there. They were in an area of derelict houses awaiting demolition to allow the estate to be extended. All around were shuttered windows and piles of litter and debris. The dog's inquisitive nature and strong desire to feel human fingers scratch the back of his ear urged him to move forward. He stood up, took a few short steps and sat down again. There was no encouragement from the stranger, nor any discouragement. She stared straight at him. The dog wasn't sure. He couldn't read the signs so he hesitated.

Belinda blinked rapidly. Her heart hammered alarmingly, pumping the blood faster and faster around her arteries. Droplets of sweat ran over her scalp like tiny creatures scampering among the hair roots. She saw the leathery-skinned vulture sitting close beside her and the fear acted as an adrenalin surge and her heart pumped even harder, making her body feel as if it was being inflated to bursting point. Transparent snake-like trails began to slide across her eyeballs. She felt her skin drawn taut over expanding bones. An all-enveloping sensation of terror squeezed her brain as if it was a wet sponge and all her memories of a past life were being wrung from it. They tumbled out in kaleidoscopic confusion, a stream of half-forgotten faces and places and whispered words. Her fear came from the fact that she knew the process was a finite one and when the

23

memories ended the darkness would inevitably follow. The pressure was unrelenting.

She looked on through a mist of superficial pain. The vulture surveyed her with a cold eye. She called it a vulture yet it had no feathers and if there were wings, they were folded tight against its scaly back. As she watched it seemed to sprout and then lose patches of coarse hair. The savagely hooked beak shape-shifted into a snarling snout crammed with jagged teeth and dripping with blood-flecked saliva. Then it was once more a smoothly curved instrument of death and dismemberment. The beast's fierce talons momentarily became fur-wrapped paws that she could imagine darting out to slash her face, then they were talons again, curling closed, sinking deep into her throat.

Rex moved a little further forward, shuffling on his bottom. He lowered his head and whined softly. His need for human affection was overcoming his innate caution. When he was not rebuked he moved even further, his head only a few inches above the ground. He nuzzled one of the stranger's hands, burrowing his nose under it and trying to flick it up so that it would pat his head. He licked the back of the hand but it remained heavy and unresponsive.

Belinda was an infant again, a small raw-fleshed baby with arms and legs coiled into an untidy bundle. The image, repeated endlessly like the frames of a reel of film, slid over both her eyes. And combined with it was another image of her mother's face bearing down on her. And through the pictures she could see the vulture, eyes sparkling with viciousness, move closer to her until with a shake of its head it tore open her hand and her arm and its teeth clamped onto her neck, chewing on the arteries there. Terror raced to a mind-shearing climax. But as the blood flowed from her bloated body the pressure inside her skull eased and, perversely, she suddenly felt calm and comfortable. Her mother's damp lips were pressed against her forehead. There was no pain any more, no fear. Her idea of herself as a new-born baby was the most beautiful thing in the world. She closed her eyes to savour it more intensely and, just for an instant as the darkness closed in, the terror returned. She opened her eyes but she could see nothing through a liquid blanket of blackness. Her brain had been squeezed dry. There was nothing left in it. She was dead.

24

Rex whined and backed off. He could not understand why the stranger did not react. The dog sat for a long time looking at her face. He saw the expression change, the edges of the mouth turn down, the twitching of the fingers become frantic and then stop, the eyes bulge and then grow dim. He waited, not knowing what to expect. Eventually his patience ran out. His stomach told him that he needed something to eat and he knew that if he was at the bus terminus on the housing scheme at a certain time there was a good chance he would get the crusts of the driver's sandwiches. Rex whined one last time. Then he left the stranger where she sat and trotted away.

7

Monday: 15.22

The central square room of the mortuary had four stainless-steel dissection platforms on it, like the skeletons of snooker tables in a deserted playing saloon. There were mirrors but no windows and all illumination was concentrated in one corner where the dead girl from the cemetery was laid out, turned over onto her back and half covered by a grey sheet that matched the depressing colour of the bare walls. The pathologist, Dr Tony Thomson, was bent over her, knife in hand, head-mounted microphone curling round to his mouth. From where he stood outside the heavy rubbery swing doors, Fyfe could see the pathologist's lips moving underneath the face mask, recording the literature of another, as yet, unexplained death. Beside him two assistants went through their own carefully choreographed movements to the constant sound of water drumming on hollow steel sinks. Thomson delved inside the chest cavity of the corpse, picked something black and shiny out and held it close to his face. He talked to it and turned to slide it into a specimen jar.

Fyfe leaned casually against the door jamb, looking through the scratched and slightly dull clear plastic of the rectangular porthole. He had no desire to get any closer to see the redundant and decomposing interior biology of the girl's body. He had seen too many post-mortems, heard the brittle snap of long-handled pincers cutting through too many ribs. He preferred to wait and watch from a decent distance so that at least he did not have to stuff cotton wool up his nostrils to stave off the nausea associated with formaldehyde-laced air and the systematic deconstruction of the interior workings of what was once a live human being.

There was a blue tinge to what he could see of the dead skin under the eerie lighting; a sharp contrast to the rosy pink bloom he remembered on Hilary's warm flesh in the pool only a few hours earlier. Fyfe wondered once more who the dead girl was and where she had come from, what kind of life she had led before it ended at the weekend. The really sad thing was that there would be other girls on the table after her, girls and young men who were even now drawing breath, experiencing the tingle of circulating blood, and believing themselves immortal.

Fyfe waited while the pathologist went about his macabre business. He had come to the mortuary too early in order to keep away from the office and avoid having to speak to anyone. He amused himself by lighting matches, holding them between two fingers and flicking the end with his thumb to snuff out the flame and create an obituary puff of smoke. He had gone through a whole box before Thomson finally emerged. He was holding something soft and glistening in his hand and Fyfe thought at first it must be an internal organ, then realized it was just the pair of unrolled rubber gloves. Thomson stood on the pedal of a waste bin, tossed the gloves inside and nodded an acknowledgement of Fyfe's existence before beginning to wash his hands. His apron was streaked with brown and grey lines and shone in the light. The microphone and face mask hung down around his neck.

'How do, Chief Inspector,' he said.

'I do fine,' Fyfe replied. 'What's the verdict?'

'Jury's still out, I'm afraid. It's a curious one. No injuries or hidden diseases or bursting aneurysms. This girl was as healthy as a horse before something happened to her which deprived her brain of oxygen. I don't think it's a regular drug overdose. There are no signs of needle marks and the initial tests suggest no presence of common drugs. So we can rule out heroin, cocaine, temazepam, ecstasy, all the stuff you normally find that fries the brain. It's quite fascinating actually.'

'What are you telling me, Doctor?'

Thomson frowned and dried his hands on a sheaf of paper towels. He had a faraway look in his eyes. His forehead had creased into a dozen deep lines and he had caught the side of his lower lip between his teeth. He was concentrating hard, examining the scientific options of the case on one intellectual level while talking to Fyfe on another.

'On a purely mechanical basis she died of respiratory failure.'

'And what induced the respiratory failure?'

'Poison, Chief Inspector.'

'Poison.'

'Our victim was poisoned by something that inhibited her ability to breathe.'

'With what?'

'I won't know until I've run more tests.'

'How long will that take?'

'As long as it takes to find out. Depends what it is. There will be traces in the blood or in the hair and I'll have to cross refer its chemical structure with the National Poisons Register. It could be a few days before we get a match.'

'Any theories to be going on with?'

Thomson blew out his cheeks and moved the bubble of air from side to side inside his mouth with a popping noise. 'It could turn out to be a cocktail of household cleaners or something equally banal, but I fancy it could be more exotic than that. You see, most poisons are easily detectable because they operate by either destroying vital organs or by impairing biological function. Whatever, it's fairly obvious once you cut a person open because you can see the damage. Drugs are a form of poison which damage the body, and they can range from the socially acceptable alcohol to totally unacceptable heroin. That, however, is not a scientific classification. An overdose of alcohol will kill you as surely as an overdose of heroin.'

'What's special about the poison in this case?'

'Here I believe we have a neural poison, a substance that effectively closed down the respiratory system, starving the brain of oxygen and causing death. Now many poisons affect the

27

brain, alcohol does of course, but it is not that reaction which kills you. It just makes you stagger about and act in various ways you would not consider when sober.'

'I know the feeling,' Fyfe said.

'Then there are nerve gases which are much favoured by the military.'

'She might have been gassed then?'

Thomson frowned more deeply and slapped his hands gently against his face. 'Conceivably, but there would probably have been signs of it in her oesophagus. However, who knows what they are turning out in our chemical weapons factories these days.'

'Are you serious?'

'Not wholly,' Thomson admitted. 'If she is a victim of poison gas how come the whole city isn't dead beside her. It's much more likely to be something she swallowed or absorbed through the skin.'

Fyfe was almost disappointed. 'So, as we stand, we still don't know if it was murder or suicide?'

'Afraid not. When I do identify the poison I still won't be able to say whether she took it willingly or if it was forced on her. That will be your job.'

'We don't even know her name yet.'

'Have you asked her boyfriend? His name is Bruce.'

'How do you know she had a boyfriend?'

'That's the name tattooed on her right buttock. I presume Bruce knew her reasonably well.'

'Show me.'

Fyfe took a deep breath and held his hand over his mouth as he followed Thomson through the swing doors into the examination room. The formaldehyde seeped through and the nausea began to fill his gullet. Thomson lifted the sheet and pushed the stiff body up to reveal the tattoo on a buttock flattened out by its contact with the solid steel surface. It was a small pink heart, rather delicately drawn, with the name Bruce printed on a ribbon that was wrapped round it.

'Very tasteful,' Fyfe said.

'Isn't it. I've already had pictures taken of it for you. They're being developed.'

They left the room again and Thomson began to divest himself of the heavy apron. Fyfe, relieved that he at least had one extra piece of information to justify his afternoon, took the opportunity to end the conversation and leave. Outside, a steady drizzle was falling. He wondered about Bruce and what the girl had talked about with the tattooist as she lay, face down, while he performed his art, unaware that later she would be found dead lying in the same position beside a toppled stone angel. At least it was a hard fact and a round of the tattoo shops should produce somebody who remembered carrying out such a task. Then they would have her name at least and the story would begin to unravel. What seemed a great mystery would become a simple explanation.

Fyfe's mobile phone rang at that moment. It was Bill Matthewson, sounding very very far away.

'We've found another dead girl,' he said and the gritty rain was suddenly running over Fyfe's face like slugs trailing acid.

8

Monday: 18.59

Fyfe arrived home more than three hours late. The after images of the young girl's body in the cemetery and the second girl at the back of the derelict block on the housing estate would not fade. They had a name for the second one, Belinda Struthers, which gave them a starting point. She had been found by a gang of kids coming out of school, sitting propped up against a graffiti scarred wall. They had assumed she was a junkie all woozy from shooting up and hadn't realized she was dead until she failed to react to the stones they threw at her. A sharp edge had cut open her forehead but no blood had flowed, no bruise had formed. Then they ran home and the police moved in. Fyfe had crouched down beside her, staring into the dead pools of her half-closed eyes, trying to see the last thing she had seen when she was alive. Similar jeans, similar anorak, similar hairstyle, but otherwise no reason to link her to the cemetery. No marks on the body, he noted. No needle holes. Another poison victim, he assumed, this time on the other side of the city. At the mortuary Tony Thomson would talk to himself behind his mask as he slid more glistening black things into jars and confirmed the cause of death.

Fyfe stood up and back from the front line of the investigation, organized a pair of detectives to begin checking tattoo shops the next day and collected all the paperwork that he was supposed to have read for his hostage negotiation course.

He had not phoned in to check that Kate had arrived safely, assuming that Sally would have contacted him if there was anything to report. He had thought about phoning just before he set out from the city, but he was already overdue by then and decided it was just as well to wait that little longer. Now he was regretting his failure to show a decent interest in the homecoming of his only daughter. He didn't have a reasonable excuse. He should have made the time. People died every day, after all, victims of a variety of ills ranging from an axe in the skull to simple, uncomplicated old age or bursting blood vessels. It was just that the girl lying prone beside the fallen angel had somehow got to him, and then the other girl with her legs splayed out in front of her and her head hanging down had made it worse. They were both somebody's daughter and they would never be going home.

Impatience with his selfish behaviour compounded with a genuine desire to see Kate and made him hurry. He turned into the driveway, manoeuvring the big estate car at speed through the narrow gap and nosing it up behind Sally's car. As he walked towards the house he rehearsed his story; a nasty murder, only senior investigating officer available, no option, got away as soon as possible. Keep it short and simple, he told himself. Don't make too big a thing out of it. Just state it and leave it. Sally wouldn't believe him anyway, and she was right. He could have got away hours before. The future of civilization didn't depend on him sitting at his desk waiting for other people to do their work and fill in their forms.

The dogs, Jill and Number Five, met him at the door and he knew then there was something wrong in the house. They didn't jump at him excitedly or shove their muzzles into his hands as

30

they usually did. Instead, it was a token welcome. They trotted up to him, brushed against his legs, turned and went back down the hall into the living room. Fyfe was seized by a sense of foreboding, similar to the one he had experienced as he crouched over the girl's body in the cemetery that morning. It bear-hugged his chest and made the blood roar in his ears. Something unpleasant lurked ahead and there was going to be no way to avoid it.

He followed the dogs. Sally and Kate were sitting side by side on the sofa. Sally looked up and he saw the anger in her eyes. She had her arm round her daughter's shoulders. Kate had her head bowed and her hands tightly clasped. Jill and Number Five sat on the floor directly in front of her staring at her tangled hair. Fyfe couldn't see Kate's face but he knew she was crying.

'What's the matter?' he asked limply.

'Good of you to make the time to come and see us,' Sally said, the sarcasm of the words sizzling like water dropped on a hotplate.

'Sorry. I got held up.'

'That's all right then.'

'What's the matter?' he asked again.

Sally got to her feet and stood directly in front of him, her face only a few inches from his. He could see that she had been crying too. The tears were still wet on her skin. The bear-hug of anxiety tightened its grip. He took a step backwards to create some space for himself.

'Don't, Mum,' Kate said from her sitting position.

'Don't what?' Sally challenged her. 'Don't hit him? Why not? Why shouldn't I hit him? Doesn't he deserve it?'

Sally punched Fyfe's arm. When he didn't react she punched him again, much harder. The third time he caught her fist in the palm of his hand and held onto it. Fresh tears were flowing. Fyfe realized that something very, very bad must have happened. He wrapped his arms round Sally and held her against him. She tried to pull away but abruptly gave in. If he hadn't been holding her she would have fallen down.

'Your son-in-law is a wife beater,' Sally said in a flat monotone drained of all emotion. 'He is a violent bastard who regularly kicks and punches our daughter to gain some kind of perverted satisfaction. And to make matters worse Kate is now pregnant.'

31

When Kate raised her head to look across he saw the bruising on her face and, for a few seconds, he thought he was going to faint. Everything around him became a featureless blur and then slowly swam back into focus. Number Five stretched her head forward and rested it on Kate's knee. Jill made a sort of half-bark, half-whine noise and pawed the air pathetically. Fyfe felt very cold. His felt his skin congeal all over, harden, as if he was turning to stone.

'I'm sorry, Dad,' Kate said.

'Don't apologize,' Sally almost shouted. 'It's not your fault.'

Sally went back to her place on the sofa beside Kate. Fyfe sat down on the other side. The three of them hugged. Fyfe didn't trust himself to speak. He buried his face in Kate's hair. His emotions were supercharged with a frightening intensity. He was paralysed by an avalanche of memories of Kate as an innocent little girl with her hair tied in bunches playing with her dolls. Holidays in the sun, playing naked on the beach, skinning her knee when she fell off her bike, dripping hot tears against his neck as he comforted her.

'Sorry, Dad,' she whispered to him so that Sally didn't hear.

9

Monday: 19.15

Katherine Leboda swept the litter of cans and cartons off the table into the black bin bag. She held it up in her fist and spun it to close the neck. Then she went to the door at the end of the carriage and threw it onto the pile of bags on the dimly lit platform. That was it, she thought gratefully. The job had not taken as long as expected so she would be able to get home quicker and still earn the extra overtime. She was glad of that because it had been a long boring day and she was looking forward to putting her feet up in front of a good film from the video shop.

The train was standing at a side platform at King's Cross

Station. It had been taken out of service because of a fault with its heating system and it was only late in the day that they had managed to fix it and then rescheduled it as one of the cross-border expresses for the early morning runs the next day. The train was in the process of being cleaned when, as soon as it was taken off the timetable, its cleaners were redeployed onto short-haul trains. When it was restored to the timetable there was a sudden panic to find somebody to finish the job. Leboda had put in eight hours and had her coat on and was halfway out of the door when her supervisor, Desmond Grainger, asked if she was interested in overtime. A widow, with teenage sons she seldom saw except at meal times, she didn't have a good excuse for turning the offer down so she accepted and used her bargaining power to negotiate a generous three hours for a job she knew would take just over one. Grainger was a pushover, shuffling towards retirement with a look of permanent bemusement on his ugly face under the mop of salt-and-pepper grey hair. She was determined to have his job once he went and she would never allow the cleaners to get away with little strokes like the one she had pulled. In the end, the carriages were not in a bad condition at all. Passengers from the north could be very messy, but not this time. It took her less than the hour she had expected.

Grainger was approaching her now. There was one difficulty. The toilet in the fourth carriage was stuck on engaged but that was probably a legacy of the problem with the electrics. She told Grainger as he came towards her and he looked at her in exaggerated shock as if she had just made an obscene suggestion. He did tend to get things out of proportion.

'Oh God, oh God,' he said, taking little steps as if he was doing a silent tap dance. 'The engineers have all gone. What will we do?'

Leboda contemplated him with barely disguised contempt. There had been a rumour a few years back that Grainger was actually a rich eccentric who only worked on the railways for a laugh. She didn't believe it but at least it would explain why he was in the job when he was so incompetent. Maybe he paid the bosses to be allowed to dick around so hopelessly.

'The shift comes in tomorrow before the train is due to leave,' she said. 'They can repair it then.'

'Of course, of course. I'd better take a look though. Just check. Which one is it?'

He started along the platform, forcing Leboda to follow him past the open doors and catch up with him and steer him into the right carriage. Grainger pressed the door opening button and bent down to inspect it more closely when nothing happened. He hammered on the door, loudly demanding to know if there was anyone inside.

'I've tried that,' Leboda informed him impatiently. 'The thing's broken, I tell you.'

'I'll use my special key,' he said.

Leboda stood back to let him open the panel covering on the control box beside the door. He inserted the metal spanner key and the red light of the engaged sign flickered slightly. The door hummed but remained firmly closed.

'Did it move?' he asked.

Leboda had seen it move a little. A tiny gap had appeared but then closed again. It didn't matter because the engineers would be available to fix it tomorrow. She wanted to get to the video shop before it rented out all the best films.

'Try the key again,' she told him in spite of herself.

Grainger turned the key. The door slid open a quarter of an inch, jerked and moved another half inch. Grainger got his fingers into the space and pulled. With another jerk the door opened all the way to reveal the body lying awkwardly on the floor in the cramped interior.

'Oh shit, oh shit, oh shit,' Grainger said, standing back and crossing himself before clamping his hand over his mouth. 'He's dead, he's dead, he's dead.'

Leboda stepped past him and looked down on the young man's curled body with his trousers round his ankles. He was not much older than her own sons. Such a handsome boy, she thought, and how embarrassed he would have been if he had known he would be found in such a position. She noticed the freshly bleeding wound on his scalp where the open- ing door had torn out a clump of hair. Grainger was mumbling about junkies and dead spirits that can enter your body through your ears or your mouth. She took charge of the situation, dropping to her knees and putting two fingers on the boy's throat, searching for a pulse. Her late husband had been a paramedic and a good one. He had taught her a lot. Where there's life, there's hope, had been one of his favourite sayings.

'Get a doctor,' Leboda shouted. 'He's still alive.'

'He's dead,' Grainger insisted. 'Dead, dead, dead.'

Leboda used all her strength to twist the boy into a position where his head was accessible. She began to give him the kiss of life, counting the rhythm. One, two, three, breathe. Move away. One, two, three, breathe. Move away. One, two, three, breathe. The boy's lips were cold but she could feel warm air inside his mouth. She would save him.

'Dangerous, dangerous,' Grainger said. 'You shouldn't be doing that.'

Leboda lifted her head. 'He's not dead. Call an ambulance, will you. Get help. We can save him.'

It probably was dangerous, she realized. She had no idea what the boy was suffering from or what had happened to him. Most likely a drug overdose, she supposed. But she made a point of acting towards others as she hoped they would act towards her. It was a simple creed she tried to live by. Besides she was fit and healthy and she was also a mother. If it was her boy she would want someone to help him. So she continued with the kiss of life. One, two, three, breathe. Move away. One, two, three, breathe. Move away.

Grainger had finally gone to fetch help. She would save him. They might even give her a medal or a good citizenship award. It would be a good way to round off a long day.

10

Monday: 21.03

Father and daughter sat side by side on the hillside above the house. The day was cooling rapidly. The insect-flecked air was turning grey around them, black on the horizon. A stiff breeze streamed over their faces and through their hair, padding out the zipped-up waxed jackets they wore. Fyfe held Kate's hand. She rested her head on his shoulder. Jill lay at their feet licking her paws. Her offspring, Number Five, was excitedly following the scent of a rabbit over the coarse grass and clumps of gorse and heather.

They could both see Sally, hundreds of yards away in the back garden. She had been watering the flowers with a hose, now she was pacing the lawn occasionally stabbing a trowel into an eruption of dandelion leaves or the soil of the flower beds alongside it. Sally always turned to gardening in times of tension. It used to be a family joke: a good display of flowers meant Mum and Dad were giving each other a hard time; an unkempt, colourless garden meant everything was sweetness and light.

The silence on the hillside was strained and awkward. The walk had been Kate's idea. She obviously wanted to get Fyfe on his own, away from Sally. She needed to talk to her father, the way she had done as an innocent child asking daft questions like why is the sky blue and why doesn't it fall on our heads. Sally had no patience with things like that. Fyfe did, although he wasn't sure he provided the right answers. Then she came to him again as a precocious teenager when the mother-daughter relationship was fraying at the edges. She didn't tell him everything, of course, but she had always been able to talk to him easily. He was a good listener. Now he was waiting for her to tell him something, unsure whether he should initiate the conversation or simply wait until she was ready to begin. He waited, stroking her hair at the back of her neck and squeezing her hand, wishing he could soothe away the pain the way he used to do before she became a woman who no longer needed him to perform fake miracles.

'Dad?'

'Mmmm?'

'You never liked Doug, did you?'

This was the beginning. This was how she began her confessions to him, never looking him in the eye, never having to check if he was actually listening. She knew he would be. She was his daughter after all. The dead girls in the cemetery and on the

36

housing scheme would have fathers somewhere too. Perhaps they were missing their daughters wondering what had happened to them. But they had suddenly grown into big girls who liked to keep secrets, so father could only hope for the best. There was little else a father could reasonably do. Daughters had their own lives to get on with, even if the pair Fyfe had seen today didn't have them any more.

'You never liked him, did you?' she asked again, demanding that he give an answer.

'Not a lot,' he replied honestly.

'I should have paid more attention to you.'

How often had he told her that, that she should listen to her world-weary father. If he could have run Kate's life it would have been so perfect for her. She would have had everything he wanted for her, and more besides, and no one would have dared to harm her. It was impossible for him to run her life, of course. It was against the laws of nature. Little girls became women and little boys became men. That was the way of it, if people lasted long enough. There were no backwaters to hide in where time stood still and nothing ever changed. In the end, everyone had to work out things on their own and take the consequences when, or if, they fucked up.

Number Five raised a rabbit from the gorse. Its white tail bobbed down the hillside with the dog in pursuit. Jill lifted her head to watch. The rabbit seemed to be running at three-quarter pace, well within its capacity. Number Five was flat out but made no impression on the gap between them. The rabbit bounced over the ground with innate natural elegance, effortlessly staying a few yards in front of the panting dog.

'Why didn't you like him?'

'Hard to say. I did try. I failed.'

It was true he had never taken to Doug as a son-in-law. There was no rational explanation for it. He just hadn't liked the man from the moment he set eyes on him. It wasn't just the natural resentment a father felt against the person who was taking his daughter away from him, it went much deeper than that. He had always thought there was something strange about Doug, something not quite right. He was not the kind of person you would meet in a pub and enjoy a drink with, though, God knew, Fyfe had tried his best. He had tried to convince himself that the problem was just Doug's nervousness, or immaturity, or stupidity. But it had seemed worse than that. He had sensed a streak of hidden malevolence. The dogs had sensed it too. More than once the birse rose on their necks when Doug appeared. But the dogs, like Fyfe, had been forced to tolerate him for Kate's sake. She was a grown woman after all. If only the three of them hadn't been so indulgent. They should have chased him away, protected their little girl. They hadn't and the shame and the guilt was a sour taste in Fyfe's mouth.

A slow-burning anger began to creep over Fyfe, its physical manifestation a rise in body temperature causing a sticky sweatiness and slight trembling as if he had a fever. He clenched his free hand and hoped Kate wouldn't notice. Sweat trickled down his spine and over his legs, quickly turning cold and forming a layer between his clothes and his skin. He pictured Doug's inanely grinning face in front of him and he pictured himself smashing his fist again and again into the smile of the bastard who had hurt his precious daughter.

'When did he first hit you?' Fyfe asked.

'We had been married three months,' Kate said evenly. 'We had been arguing. I had made a half-hearted attempt to hit his arm. He punched me on the side of the head, knocked me over.'

Fyfe did some mental arithmetic. 'That was three years ago. Why didn't you tell us?'

'I don't know. He was so apologetic the next day, couldn't do enough for me. It was another six months before he did it again. He punched me but this time he kicked me in the ribs when I fell down.'

Fyfe's stomach lurched as though he had gone over a humpbacked bridge at speed. He stared at the ground and felt the heat of his anger being translated into a paradoxical cold that wrapped his whole body. Number Five trotted back, having lost her race with the rabbit. She sat down and began to lick a front paw like a cat.

Kate laughed humourlessly. 'I should have left him then, but he could be so pathetically sorry. He agreed to seek help, went for counselling, saw a psychiatrist. They told him he was responding well but he was still hitting me. It was never too bad,

38

just the odd kick or punch. I never had serious black eyes or bruising that showed or anything like that.'

'Three years.' Fyfe shook his bowed head sadly. 'You had three years of it.'

'I phoned Mum a couple of times but I didn't have the courage to tell her. I had this queer idea it was somehow my fault. Doug was ill, you see, and I had to make allowances.'

'No illness has symptoms that include beating women.'

'It got worse,' Kate went on as if she hadn't heard. 'The kicks and punches became more frequent and Doug got sicker. The doctors said he had a mild form of schizophrenia and prescribed some kind of tranquillizers. I'm not so sure about the mild. At the start of the year he gave up his job, just walked out one day. He started working as a barman in a really seedy bar. We didn't have enough money to pay the mortgage. When I confronted him he curled up into a ball at my feet and held onto my legs. It took me half an hour to prise him off. It was scary.'

'Why didn't you tell us what was going on?'

'I couldn't, Dad. I'm sorry.' She was crying openly. The darkness fell around them. 'It was my problem. Doug said he was hearing voices and that the voices were telling him I was being unfaithful.'

'Why didn't you just leave him?'

'I don't know.'

Fyfe tightened his grip on Kate's hand. It was such a stupid thing to do, offer simple solutions to a horribly complicated situation, but he couldn't help himself. Life was never simple. Love was never straightforward. People were so dumb, believing they could control the course of events. They couldn't.

'There's something else I want to tell you, Dad.'

'What?'

'Doug was right.'

'What do you mean?'

'His voices were telling him the truth. It's not his baby.'

Fyfe was mildly surprised rather than shocked. He absorbed the information and pulled Kate closer to him in an unconscious gesture of congratulations. If Doug wasn't the father he had no rights over the baby. Kate could make a

39

clean break. There would be no custody battle or anything like that.

'No? Then whose?'

'A friend.'

'I see. Does he know?'

'Who? Doug or the father?'

'Doug.'

'Doug would never believe he isn't the father, but he isn't. We hadn't slept together, you know properly, for ages. That was why he hit me that last time. I wouldn't have sex with him. It made him angry.'

'What about the real father?'

'He doesn't know.'

'Are you going to tell him?'

'I doubt it.'

Fyfe hesitated, wondering what to say next. Kate rested her head on his shoulder and he patted her with his free hand, trying to soothe away all the pain and the confusion.

'Tell me about him.'

'He's married.' She giggled. 'Well, not really. Separated. We met at a party, would you believe. Eyes across a crowded room. That's how it started. Our affair lasted about six or seven months. In fact, we have a date arranged for tonight but he'll be stood up. He'll wonder where I am.'

Like father, like daughter, Fyfe thought. He had discovered Hilary in a crowded room, though any affair between them had yet to begin properly. However, the invitation had now very definitely been extended and he fully intended to accept it.

'Do you love him?' Fyfe asked.

'Maybe. I only used him for affection because of what was happening between me and Doug but it got to be more than that.'

'Forget him. Sally and I will look after you. You are going to keep your baby?'

'Oh yes.'

'Good.'

'Is it? Is it good?'

'I think so. Alive is better than dead, don't you think?'

40

'Sometimes. Don't tell Mum about the baby's father. I haven't told her yet. I want to pick the right moment.'

Fyfe got up and helped Kate to her feet. The house below them was an island of light in deep waters of darkness. The wind brushed their faces. The dogs stretched and trotted downhill ahead of them.

'Would I like him, Kate? The father of my first grandchild?'

She thought about it for a while. 'Yes,' she said finally. 'You would like him.'

'But I'm never going to meet him?'

'No.'

'It's probably for the best.'

11

Monday: 23.52

Scott Anderson was nudged awake by the sharp point of his wife's elbow. He ignored it at first but she was insistent, finally resorting to taking hold of a fold of flesh at his waist and squeezing until the discomfort grew to be too much and he could only get relief by rolling over onto his back. It was the middle of the night. She hadn't seemed particularly randy earlier on. Why was she suddenly demanding sex now? What was she on?

'For fuck's sake, woman,' he complained. 'I was sound asleep. What's the matter with you?'

Even as he spoke he was becoming aware that something was wrong in the bedroom. He saw that Margaret was sitting up, her body unnaturally rigid, her head pressed against the wall as if an invisible hand had her by the throat. The bedside lamp was on with a cloth draped over it to soften the output of light. It had the effect of turning Margaret's face into a shadow-drawn horror mask. Anderson's movements were already slow, but instinctively he slowed them further lest he attract unwanted attention to himself as he raised his head from the pillow and looked down the bed to the spot where Margaret's eyes were fixed. It

41

was only then that he noticed the sound, a low guttural buzzing that reminded him of the noise made by a wasp trapped in a jam jar. The buzzing sound was increasing in intensity, becoming louder and more threatening, more sinister. Anderson blinked to clear his sleep-stuck eyes and made out his pet dog sitting at the bottom of the bed. The dog's eyes glowed red in the dim light and the whiteness of his teeth glinted where the lip was curled back in a vicious snarl.

Anderson experienced a sense of disorientation and relief. The adrenalin that had pumped itself into his blood rapidly dissipated. He had braced himself to expect something fearsome and alarming. Instead it turned out to be that stupid mongrel Rex he would have got rid of long ago if he had been allowed to have his way. There he sat, growling and dripping gobs of saliva onto the covers.

'Get off the bed, Rex,' he shouted. 'What the fuck do you think you're playing at? You know you're not allowed on our bed.'

The dog did not move. The pitch of the growl went up two octaves. The lip curled higher, revealing yellowy-pink gums as well as starkly white teeth. Margaret seized his arm and dug in her fingernails painfully.

'I said get off the fucking bed.'

Anderson swung a kick at Rex but his foot was held back by the tucked-in blankets. It ended up as nothing more than a gentle pat on the dog's chest. He kicked again but the result was the same. He sat up and leaned forward, punching out in an effort to dislodge the dog. As his hand touched its fur the steady drone of the threatening growl was transformed into a short outburst of savage barking. In the silence that followed Anderson pulled back his hand and he and Margaret looked with detached surprise at the freshly red twin tracks on his wrist and forearm where the dog's teeth had sunk in and torn the flesh. The pain was delayed, gradually building and asserting itself, not enough yet to cause him to cry out. He lifted his eyes and glared accusingly at the dog on the bed. Rex, the cute little mongrel with the endlessly wagging tail, gave a single warning snarl and launched himself at his master's throat.

Margaret screamed and scrambled out of the bed. Anderson managed to get his arms up in time to deflect the main force of the lunge but Rex was on top of him and his front and rear claws were scraping for a grip on his bare chest. Teeth snapped and slashed at the exposed blood vessels in Anderson's neck. He held the dog in a bear-hug and desperately tried to work out what to do. He winced as the flesh on his shoulder was ripped by a sideways jerk of the slavering jaws, and then again as his cheek was bitten. He rolled over onto his front, using his weight to flatten the dog against the mattress. He noticed that it had become partially entangled in the covers so he rolled over again and it was more tightly restrained. Margaret was shouting to him from the floor, telling him to run. He jumped up on his knees and bundled the furiously writhing body in a mess of twitching blankets. He held it for a few seconds but quickly realized it was going to twist itself free, so he heaped more blankets on top and ran for the door, grabbing Margaret on the way. He made it with seconds to spare, slamming the door shut and leaning back against it. Inside the bedroom, Rex, barking and snarling, thumped against the solid door in a futile attempt to get at him.

Anderson was covered in his own blood. He held out his hands in a gesture of helplessness. Margaret was standing in front of him offering him a roll of kitchen paper to wipe the wounds and a big bath towel to wrap himself in. Somehow during the panic she had managed to put on a dressing gown and slippers and with them an expression of surprised bewilderment.

'I've called an ambulance, Scott,' she announced. 'You're a mess. You'll have to go to hospital.'

12

Tuesday: 08.10

Mother and daughter were up very early, whispering together in hushed tones in the kitchen, head to head across the table, both cradling in their hands mugs of hot coffee that grew cold without being drunk. Girl talk.

43

Kate was on her way back to bed when Fyfe stumbled downstairs with the dogs running around his legs. She kissed him on the cheek in passing but said nothing beyond a cheery good morning. Sally ran him to the airport to catch the London shuttle. It was a cold morning with a cold sun climbing into the bottom corner of a steely grey sky, leaving a film of white rime on the roadside fields and verges. They drove in silence, Fyfe dozing fitfully in the artificial warmth of the car, wondering how much Sally now knew about the circumstances of Kate's baby.

'What are we going to do about our little girl?' Sally asked suddenly.

Fyfe opened his eyes and came awake. They were on the airport slip road in a slow-moving queue of traffic. Exhausts belched clouds of vanishing vapour. Brake lights shone bright red and then faded to dull, like small fires struggling to catch hold and burn.

'We take care of her,' he replied.

'I suppose we do. Has she told you about the baby?'

Fyfe glanced sideways and nodded. Sally's expression was strained. Her hair was swept back and tied tightly, locking behind it all the hurt and anger she was containing with difficulty. They had talked briefly in bed before falling asleep and the morning rush had offered no opportunity for reasoned discussion at any length. But words between them were for confirmation because they had been together long enough for each to know what the other was thinking. Unqualified support for their daughter. She was not to blame. The disowned son-in-law Doug was to blame and therefore, by association, every man. Fyfe knew the way Sally's mind worked and judged it better for him to keep quiet.

'Did she tell you who the father was?'

'No.'

'She's not going to have anything to do with him, is she? That's what she told you. Whoever he is.'

'Doesn't look like it.'

Sally thought deeply, tapping her fingers impatiently on the steering wheel and frowning so that the skin crinkled into a hundred tiny lines at the corners of her eyes. Fyfe felt the familiar twinge of affection for her born of long association. Their lives had been inextricably bound together for so long, yet their entire mutual history could be passed inside his head in the space of only a few seconds. They met, they married, they lost the place, they divorced, they reconciled and intended to re-marry soon although they kept putting the actual date off. That was it neatly encapsulated and sealed off from other tangential episodes that would take in his heavy drinking, his womanizing, and his hypocritical flouting of the law he was employed to enforce. A few more seconds were devoted, without guilt he noticed, to the recent episode of slim-hipped Hilary pushing up on her arms to lift herself out of the swimming pool, and another few seconds each for yesterday's pair of dead girls who would never go home to cry on their parents' shoulders. There were, as the saying eternally foretold, always those worse off than your-self.

'I never liked Doug, you know,' Sally said.

'Neither did I,' Fyfe answered.

'But what can you do? Children won't listen.'

'They have to find out for themselves. It's nature's way.'

'Like we did?'

'Exactly. From now on it's damage limitation at best.'

'Yes. We'll take care of her.'

'Look on the bright side. We'll have her at home.'

'And the dogs will have somebody to play with.'

The car had reached the setting-down section of the airport terminal. Fyfe checked his watch. He was running late. He hadn't had a chance to phone in to find out if there were any developments with the girl in the cemetery and he hadn't read any of the material he was supposed to have studied for the training course. He took his overnight bag from the rear seat and leaned over to kiss Sally goodbye. She kept looking straight ahead, not acknowledging the contact.

'Why don't you visit Doug when you're down,' she said.

'Why would I want to do that?'

Sally turned her head and flashed a genuine smile that lit up her whole face. She returned the kiss.

'To kick the shit out of the little bastard,' she said. 'Why else?'

45

13

Tuesday: 09.34

Archie Irvine checked his watch and smiled smugly. The bastard Stoddart was more than half an hour late for his shift and his bus had been taken out by another driver now. Irvine was entitled to suspend him for a day without pay, and issue a written warning as to his future behaviour. He had been waiting for this chance ever since he had been promoted to depot supervisor at the start of the year. He hated Stoddart. No overt reason, it was a gut feeling. He just thought his eyes were too close together and he had an annoying, supercilious manner. Hopefully, the company would soon be able to get rid of him altogether. His attendance record was patchy and there were plenty of other good men out there willing to do his job, and do it with a better grace. Two written warnings, and the third was the sack. Goodbye Billy. I wish I could say it has been nice knowing you, but I can't.

Irvine sniffed triumphantly when he saw Stoddart enter through the big doors of the Annandale Street bus garage. The man looked the worse for drink. His clothes were dishevelled and his hair was a mess. He staggered rather than walked and his eyes were badly bloodshot. Irvine moved forward to intercept him, speaking into his handheld radio at the same time to summon a witness. Reporting for work with an illegal blood alcohol count was an immediate sacking offence. Here was an opportunity to avoid a lot of grief and a lot of paperwork and get him sacked on the spot.

'Just a minute, Billy,' Irvine said, grabbing him by the elbow. 'You're late. Your bus has already gone out. You're in trouble. What's the matter with you, man? Are you drunk?'

Stoddart's lips moved but formed no words. Irvine frowned. He didn't like what he saw, didn't like the strange threatening look in the man's eyes. It was frightening. He was like a cornered animal. Irvine backed off slowly, holding his hands up in front of him to keep Stoddart at bay. But it was a futile gesture. Stoddart charged at him, arms windmilling furiously. A fist crashed into Irvine's chin, another slammed into the side of his head, stunning him and toppling him onto the oil-stained concrete floor. The blows had drained his strength and there was nothing he could do as feet trampled over him. He was dazed, resting on one knee, when he heard the racing engine, looked up and saw the bus bearing down on him at speed. He had the presence of mind to roll to one side and the draught of the passing bulk of the bus blew against his cheek. He collapsed onto the floor again. All he could think of as he lay there was that this time Billy Stoddart had gone too far.

Billy Stoddart felled the enemy officer and climbed into the cockpit of the Lightning jet. He gunned the engine. It roared, the sound filling his head like air filling a balloon. He manoeuvred in the tight space inside the hangar until the exit came in view and he released the throttle. The jet leapt forward, bodies scattering to either side. Stoddart had always wanted to fly a Lightning since the day his father had lifted him up and lowered him into the pilot's seat at the Leuchars air show many years ago. It was a wonderful feeling to achieve his ambition. Now he would do a low-level fly-past over his home, maybe a victory roll, provided he could get through the flak the enemy would throw at him. Here it came, even as he reached the end of the runway and the powerful jet lifted into the air. He was scrabbling around trying to find his oxygen mask when the plane shuddered under the full force of a direct hit. In the fraction of a second before the irresistible forces crushed the life out of him and he lost consciousness, Stoddart congratulated himself on a good death.

Irvine was on his knees as he watched the maroon double-decker bus career through the doors of the garage, batter several cars out of the way, demolish the low perimeter wall and railings, and continue straight on to plough into the wall of the building opposite. Other people ran past him, following the runaway bus, shouting uselessly, and finally standing beside the crumpled front of the wreckage, just staring. By the time Irvine got there the line of gawping spectators was two deep. One of the first arrivals had slid open the window to try and help Stoddart out of the cab with its blood-spattered windows. But there was nothing to be done. He was very obviously dead, hanging out of the open window, his head turned entirely round so that it faced in the wrong direction. Blood trickled to the ground, pooling in plastic-like blobs. Irvine was not the only person who vomited at the sight.

'Bloody hell,' somebody said. 'What was he on?'

14

DI Connor Harper yawned and scratched the back of his neck where his tan bordered on sunburn and the skin was beginning to peel. He could still feel the heat of the Greek islands, the fine sand between his toes, and the taste of the local wine in his mouth. The charter flight had only got back in late on Monday night and he had hoped to break himself back into the old routine gently. If there hadn't been the urgent message on his answering machine, he doubted if he would have crawled out of bed yet. Instead, it was straight in at the deep end with a brain teaser about an anonymous young girl found in a cemetery with nothing to identify her but a rather fetching tattoo of a heart on her buttock which implicated an unknown man called Bruce. He examined the colour photograph. Very tasteful, he decided, thinking of Kelly's thorny rose nestling discreetly on the inside of her left thigh. Not that he had seen much of it on his two weeks' holiday because they had fallen out early on and never regained their romantic balance. They had been at each other's throats all the time and Kelly had stormed off to find her own taxi when the flight landed. God, it had been a nightmare, not exactly the relaxing experience he had hoped for. They had fought continually. At one point, in a crowded taverna, she had poured beer over his head and stormed out. Then she had gone into a frenzy when he staggered back to their room, beating him with a hair brush until he locked himself in the bathroom and slept in the bath. He still had the bruises on his back. And to make matters worse, he was hardly through his own door when his ex-wife Anne was on to him demanding to know what had happened to the agreed maintenance payments. He blamed the bank, although he knew full well that he had allowed his account to run into overdraft to pay for the holiday. Anne had slammed down the phone. He had got himself a drink and cursed womankind.

Harper started to read all the available details on the case before the inquiry team arrived and demanded to know what to do next. DCI Fyfe had left him a handwritten note: Assigned Munro and Crichton to check tattooists. Harper nodded at the wisdom of such a tactic. A door-to-door had already been done in the vicinity of the cemetery and produced nothing constructive. He would order it done again to stamp his authority on the investigation. It was an old trick and a disreputable one that made the foot soldiers think they were at fault for not turning anything up, thereby shifting the blame for lack of progress from the generals sitting in headquarters. In fact, it was Fyfe who had taught him the trick. Pity he was otherwise engaged because Harper badly needed somebody to lean on. Fyfe revelled in obscure mysteries and saw significant patterns where others saw only daft tattoos and dead flesh.

Harper breathed deeply and felt sorry for himself. The cemetery girl definitely looked like a suicide, he decided. Nothing grander than that. The unidentified toxin in her blood would confirm that theory once they discovered what it was – some curious cocktail of drugs probably. Not much of a mystery at all really. The difficulty would be in finding out who she was.

Harper reached inside his jacket pocket and took out the quarter bottle of whisky in the white paper bag he had bought at a corner shop on his way in that morning. He held it below the level of his desk, between his knees and turned it over and over in his hands. His head was sore at the prospect of Anne nipping at him when he went round to see the kids with their presents, and he knew he would have to grovel to Kelly to pacify her if he was ever to see that rose tattoo again. He took a tube of extra strong mints from his other pocket. He had bought it in the shop at the same time as the whisky, keeping his head down so that he didn't have to look the shopkeeper in the eye. No explanation was asked for and none offered. This was a very bad idea. He shouldn't be doing this, the warning voice inside his head told him, but he ignored it as he had done all his life.

He twisted the cap and it snapped free. He had nothing to pour the liquid into so, with a surreptitious glance at the closed door, he raised the bottle and drank straight from the neck. The whisky burned his mouth, soothed his head, calmed his nerves. It fortified him and made him feel able to face the world and its quaint ways. Now he felt confident he would get through the day. He wished himself back to the beach in Greece, lying under the shade with Kelly straddling him to rub oil into his pectorals. He pressed his stomach and promised himself at least two sessions in the gym every week to shed some weight. It would never happen of course but it was a reasonable ambition. He needed to make some effort to keep his young girlfriend because he didn't have the money to impress her. His baby face made him look young anyway, despite the greying hair and the estranged wife and the streetwise kids who were taller than he was now. If he kept off the beer for a while he might manage to reduce his spreading waistline. He wasn't going to eat for a while either to see if that would make any difference. He hadn't had any breakfast and he didn't feel hungry yet. That was a good sign. He took another drink and rubbed his itchy neck.

There was a knock at the door and DS Bill Matthewson put his head round. Harper dropped the whisky bottle into his lap and felt some of the spirit leak out onto his trousers. He put his hands on the desk, like a magician demonstrating he had nothing up his sleeves, and realized that he was holding the cap. He hid it by forming a fist.

'Have a good holiday, sir?' Matthewson asked.

'Great,' Harper replied. 'Only one problem with it.'

'What's that?'

'It didn't last long enough.'

Harper adjusted his legs to stop the whisky pouring out and the bottle slipped upright. He tried not to breathe in Matthewson's direction and wondered what Kelly was saying about him to her friends.

'They never do, holidays.'

'I feel renewed and revived, ready for the fray,' Harper said, hoping that he could talk himself into a more positive frame of mind. 'What are you going to tell me, Bill?'

'We got another one last night.'

'Another what?'

Matthewson walked towards the desk and let the cardboard folder he held fall open with practised efficiency. 'Another body. Another young girl. Another suspicious death. She was found late yesterday afternoon. Post-mortem will be carried out in the next few hours but the preliminary examination has produced something rather interesting.'

Harper leaned forward and read the top of the file upside down. 'This is the opposite side of the city,' he said. 'What's the link with the cemetery girl?'

'There is a cast-iron link.'

'Go on, surprise me.'

'She had a heart tattooed on her buttock. Bruce had been there too, so it seems.'

Matthewson threw down another colour photograph that landed alongside the one already on Harper's desk. Harper raised his eyebrows and touched the picture to check that the tattoo had not been superimposed as some kind of elaborate joke to welcome him back to work. He hesitated and waited for a bunch of them to come rushing in after Matthewson, laughing their heads off. Nothing happened. Matthewson stood waiting.

'This bloke Bruce gets around, doesn't he?' Harper said.

'I believe we will find the same unidentified toxin in the blood of this victim and that they died around the same time.'

'What do you think it means, Bill?'

'God knows what to think.'

'A suicide pact?' Harper speculated.

Matthewson shrugged unhelpfully. 'The city's going mad. We've just had a bus crash down in the centre. Driver went off his head and tried to run over his mates, then smashed a double-decker into a brick wall. Killed himself instantly.'

'Do we have a name for this second girl?' Harper asked.

'Belinda Struthers.'

51

'That's one hundred per cent more than we have on the cemetery girl.'

'Yes, sir. We checked her out before we found the tattoo. A local girl but in care most of her life. No parents or relatives. No friends as yet.'

'We'll need a door-to-door.'

'It's scheduled for this morning.'

'What about beside the cemetery?'

'It's been done.'

'We need to do it again. We might have missed something.'

'You're the boss.'

Matthewson left. Harper picked the bottle from between his legs and took another mouthful. He screwed the cap back on and put it into his pocket, bringing out the mints at the same time and breaking the tube open. He placed a mint on his tongue and looked down at the pair of photographs of tattooed female backsides on the desk in front of him. It was like having double vision. The mystery he thought he had solved so simply was deepening in front of his eyes. At least it gave him a direction to move in but he had a feeling this was going to be a bastard of a case. He sucked the mint and the whisky taste gradually faded.

Who could understand the quaint ways of the modern world, he wondered. Who would want to? Certainly not him.

15

Tuesday: 11.48

The nurse came into the room and did all the usual medical things around Scott Anderson's bed. He lay in a drug-induced stupor thinking how attractive she looked in her starched white uniform and trying hard to recall what had happened to him. It was a total blank.

The nurse leaned over to check that there was no leakage from any of the bandages that covered his chest, neck, face and arms. Her subtle perfume made his nostrils dilate. He wanted to speak to her but could not find his voice. He wanted to reach out and touch her but he had no strength. He wanted to warn her but he didn't know against what.

She did not move away. She kept her face within a few inches of his and her breath was warm against his eyeballs. Her tongue curved out and licked the tip of his nose. She smiled and when her lips pulled back from her teeth he saw that the canines were long and sleek and razor sharp. She pressed her thumb against the point of one tooth and the slightest touch instantly produced a tiny pearl drop of red blood that remained balanced on the skin until she sucked it clean.

She stepped back and began to undress. The white uniform came away from her shoulder first, then with a secondary movement the flesh also peeled off. The bone was exposed and the cords of red and blue blood and the muscle fibres and the stringy ligaments. She uncovered her other shoulder and her torso; the lungs and the pumping heart and all the shiny, wet internal organs. She wiggled her hips to ease off the tight-fitting skin over them, revealing the pelvis and the broad hip bones at the same time as she stripped the skin from her hands as if it was a pair of gloves. With bony fingers she pulled her face and hair off and the bulging eyes stood out from the bare skull. The crumpled body suit lay on the floor and the newly created skeletal figure of the nurse stepped out of it and came towards the bed. She leaned over Anderson and he watched in awed fascination as her tongue emerged from the grinning mask. He could see the root of her tongue, a fleshy pink mound, pulsing at the back of her throat, and the touch of its tip against his nose stung like the clinical insertion of a scalpel blade.

Anderson was unable to move. Slowly, moving stiffly and awkwardly, the skeleton nurse climbed onto the bed so that she was kneeling astride him. Her skull was lower than her raised backside. The organs inside her rippled and flexed like independent living things. He could see the blood running through her veins. Her eyeballs stared into Anderson's eyes and he remembered what had happened; how Rex had gone mad and attacked him in the bedroom. He began to sweat. The skeleton nurse dug her sharp fingers into his arms. She ran her tongue over her teeth and then bit him in the neck. The shock and the

53

delicious rush of pain made him black out as if a soft velvet blanket had been placed over his face.

When he came round his wife Margaret was standing at the foot of the bed framed against the tall window. There were tears staining her face and she was making the sign of the cross. He couldn't move, couldn't speak, couldn't hear, couldn't make himself understood. The skeleton nurse had put her body suit back on. She came up behind Margaret. Then a doctor in a white coat walked right past her and up to the side of the bed. The doctor shone a light into Anderson's face and shook his head sadly. He turned away to speak to Margaret but Anderson could not hear what was said. The doctor turned back. He pressed on Anderson's eyes with his thumb, then lifted the sheet and pulled it up and over Anderson's face.

I'm not dead, Anderson wanted to shout through the transparent shroud, but his scream was silent. He could see Margaret as a grey shape through the dazzlingly white weave of the sheet. Her head was bowed. The nurse was comforting her. The doctor too. They were huddled together, an immobile cameo at the foot of the bed, like figures arranged in a painting.

I'm not dead, Anderson wanted to say but he was aware of himself growing colder and stiffer, gradually losing feeling in his arms and legs. The cold crept over him as if ice was being packed around his body and the meltwater was flowing over him. He began to think that perhaps he really was dead. He screwed his eyes shut and with a supreme effort of will he forced his limbs to obey his brain's commands. He sat up. The sheet fell away and the plasters attaching the electrical contacts were torn from his skin. The room was empty. He got to his knees. The bed was tilting and he couldn't find any handholds. It was at a forty-five degree angle and rising steadily. He was sliding down, desperately searching for a grip. The window was open and he was falling towards it.

The nurse appeared beside him. He took hold of her wrist and stopped himself falling through the window. The glass was intensely cold against the soles of his feet, colder than ice. Then the nurse's eyes glowed red and her lip curled up, distorting her face in a terrible snarl. She bared her teeth and hissed. Anderson was surprised that he could hear the sound. All of his senses were abruptly acute. The outside world crashed into his consciousness like an explosion of shattering glass. He watched in horrified fascination as the flesh on the nurse's wrist began to give way, ripping at the joint to expose the bones and sliding off in his hand. Anderson fell off the bed, tumbling into open space, momentarily turning in mid-air and looking back at the leering face watching him from the broken window. Freezing air whistled round his falling body. He turned again and the ground was accelerating up at him, its grey bulk transforming into the likeness of the face of a giant dog with wild eyes, sharp teeth and slavering jaws leaping up and going directly for his throat. He hit the tarmac and the jaws clamped tight shut around him.

16

Tuesday: 14.26

'Hallucinations certainly. There is no question. Of what order I cannot yet say but the chemical content of the substance would indicate a quite extensive hallucinatory capability. It is not an opiate but something fairly close in purely chemical terms.'

Grant McDougall, Professor of Toxicology at Edinburgh University, frowned thoughtfully and pursed his lips behind his thick grey-flecked beard. He ran a yellow nicotine-stained finger over the sheet of paper with the results of the spectrometer tests and shook his head slightly. He had explained that they had been unable to match the compound of chemicals to any on the National Poisons Register. This was a relatively unusual occurrence given the extensiveness of the register. It was the combination of up to forty different agents in the compound that was proving hard to crack. Further investigations were under way.

Connor Harper surreptitiously wiped his nose with the back of his hand. The change in climate since coming back from Greece had made him susceptible to the cold. He could feel it coming on: the dull buzzing inside his head, the pain behind his eyes, a dryness in his mouth and throat. Of course, the alcohol might be to blame. The half-empty whisky bottle in his jacket pocket seemed inordinately heavy. It could induce hallucinations too. He had the briefest vision of his ex-wife embracing him fondly when he took the kids their presents from his holiday. And then his girlfriend prostrating herself in front of him to apologize for her behaviour. Fat chance. He turned his attention to the real world.

'Hallucinations, you say.'

'Mmmm,' McDougall replied as if he was having his own personal vision.

'And that killed them?'

'No. The poison also had the effect of depressing their respiratory function. That is what killed them.'

'They stopped breathing.'

'Precisely.'

Harper wrote the word hallucination in his notebook and drew a heart next to it. He drew an arrow piercing the heart and three droplets of blood falling towards the bottom of the page.

He had been glad to get out of the office. The inquiry had already gained its own momentum and he was content to let them get on with it. He knew they would assume he was doing something important, and being in charge meant he didn't have to explain. When he got back he could take the credit for all that had been done and criticize the incompetent bastards if it didn't take them much further forward. It was David Fyfe who had taught him that particular trick when he'd first been promoted to inspector. It seemed such a long time ago now.

'Of course,' McDougall was saying while tugging at his beard, 'the hallucinations would play an important part in the biological process that led to ultimate depression of respiratory function.'

'How do you mean?'

'If the hallucination or series of hallucinations is frightening, for example, or a manifestation of physical exertion or a burst of sheer exhilaration then the subject's pulse rate would increase, pushing up blood pressure and thereby accelerating the process that results in eventual respiratory close-down.'

'I understand,' Harper said.

'You see, Inspector, a subject can, quite literally, be terrified to death depending on the quality and content of the accompanying hallucination. It is an observed toxicological consequence, informally known as the Nightmare Syndrome. As for exhilaration, it is a variant on the same principle. The excitement kills you, shall we say.'

'And what's this with physical exertion?'

'Also observed. A subject can think he is running a marathon, or lifting a heavy weight, or making love to a beautiful woman, or indeed a number of beautiful women.'

'Christ, can that kill you as well?'

McDougall's beard expanded as his mouth spread in a wide smile to peek through the hairs. 'Oh yes, Inspector. For women it can be making love to a man, or whatever. It's quite commonly reported in non-fatal cases of such quasi-opiate overdose. You won't find it in any books but personally I call it the Shagging Syndrome. And, of course, they can be mixed up.'

'Nightmare shagging.'

McDougall raised his eyebrows in confirmation. Propriety brought a faint flush to his cheeks. He placed a cigarette in his mouth and lit it. Harper wondered if he had to stop smoking halfway down the cigarette to prevent his beard catching fire.

'Of course, we don't know for certain what goes on inside anyone's head when they approach the life-threatening extreme,' McDougall said. 'In most cases we can make an educated guess by analysing a subject's overt behaviour. Sometimes, however, this can be totally irrational and any interpretation is subjective.'

'And you've no idea what the stuff could be?'

'It has me stumped.'

'Not even a hunch? A working theory?'

'Nothing useful. I will find out, though, in time.'

Harper wrote Nightmare Shagging in his notebook and drew two stick people lying on top of each other beside it. The last droplet of blood dripping from the heart was just above them on the page. He flicked the notebook shut and put it away, feeling the touch of the solid glass of the bottle in his pocket. McDougall's cigarette had burned more than halfway down. The glowing red end was now very close to the hairs of the beard. One more inhalation, Harper thought, and the whole face would go up in flames. He was disappointed when McDougall stubbed out the cigarette and took the business card he was offering.

'Thank you, Professor,' Harper said. 'Let me know as soon as you have any more information on the poison.'

'Trust me,' McDougall said, sounding like a second-hand car salesman. 'It is yours as soon as I have it, Inspector.'

17

Tuesday: 15.01

The concrete of the platform rippled as the first shock of the earthquake hit it. Katherine Leboda, watching from inside the train carriage, grabbed onto the seat backs to steady herself. The carriage bucked, riding the solid wave that ran along the ground. She let go of the seats and dropped the rubbish bag she was carrying. She fell to her knees, crouching with her hands over her head, making herself as small as possible. The whole of King's Cross Station rocked and rattled and then settled back into place as the shock passed, leaving showers of rust and dust dribbling from the supporting girders of the roof. Pigeons flew in panicky circles and then landed and began strutting round as if nothing had happened.

Leboda crawled over the seat to the window and surveyed the scene. She was amazed to see the pigeons and the people walking about normally. It was a miracle there had been no injuries but it must have been just a small shock, preceding the massive earthquake that was to come. She had felt it building up, a low rumble in the pit of her stomach, without knowing what it was. It had gradually expanded up and out through her body so that she was literally shaking when she first saw the ground move and realized what was happening. Now it was there again, the pain in her stomach, already beginning to build. Another shock was on its way. A much bigger one this time. She had to warn everyone.

'Katherine. Is something the matter?'

She turned at the tap on her shoulder and saw the cleaning supervisor, Desmond Grainger, standing behind her. He withdrew his hand as if she had grown too hot to touch.

'We have to evacuate the station,' she said, backing off the seat and standing up beside him.

'I beg your pardon,' he said.

'We have to get the people out. There's going to be an earthquake.'

Grainger's head moved away with a jerk, as if a bottle of smelling salts had been thrust under his nose. He leaned back at an angle and held out his arms towards her. 'Are you all right, Katherine?' he asked tentatively. 'You're not making any sense.'

'Quick. It's coming soon. We have to warn everybody.'

Leboda could feel the pain inside her expanding, growing, spreading like ripples from a stone thrown into still water. She was that stone, plunging deep into Mother Earth and throwing out the destructive waves that would kill and maim unless she could prevent it. She was to blame and so she had to act. She had to do something to stop such needless loss of life. Grainger was in front of her, his expression changing from sympathetic to hostile.

'You've been acting strangely all day, Katherine. You haven't been drinking, have you?'

'It's coming. Why can't you understand?'

'Drugs? Is that it? Have you been taking drugs?'

He seized her by the upper arms and leaned forward to smell her breath. She beat her fists on his chest and twisted free, ducking and squeezing past him in the inside of the carriage. He was knocked sideways, falling over a seat with his legs raised up in the air. She ran to the door and jumped onto the platform. It was deserted. All the people were over in the main body of the station. She ran towards them, shouting. The pain inside her was getting worse all the time, like labour just before childbirth, increasing relentlessly towards an inevitable climax. She knew the earthquake was imminent. She could imagine the rippling waves of solid concrete that were following her, rearing up and bearing down on the unsuspecting crowds to smash them to bits and wash them away in the flood.

'Look out,' she screamed, waving frantically. 'Run. Get out of here. There's danger.'

People in the main concourse turned to look at her. Nobody ran. Nobody moved. She grabbed hold of a man in a long coat and shouted in his face but he swung his briefcase and brushed her off. She moved on to the next person but again was shrugged off. People ran from her. A drunk offered to dance with her. The next person she tried to grab neatly sidestepped and her momentum made her fall to her knees, sliding yards over the smooth surface. The pain was intense now. She folded her arms across her stomach and tried to hold it in but knew it was useless. She bent right over until her forehead touched the ground. Her attempts at warning were far too late. There was no way of avoiding the tragedy now. The earthquake was already in progress. The fatal concrete wave was ripping up the surrounding streets until it towered over the station, hanging briefly in the air before crashing through the roof and sweeping away everyone and everything inside it, including her, in a maelstrom of noise and flailing rag-doll limbs.

Nobody went near Leboda's crouching body for a couple of minutes. They stood around in a circle waiting for her to get up and continue the performance. It was Grainger who eventually arrived and felt obliged to go to her, kneeling down, murmuring 'Oh shit, oh shit, oh shit' as he reached out with a trembling hand to put two fingers on the throat pulse just as he had seen her do with the boy in the train toilet the day before. He looked up at the ring of blank faces. He couldn't find a pulse.

18

Tuesday: 18.30

Fyfe left his London hotel and walked along Tottenham Court Road. It was newly washed by a shower of rain but it still smelled of oil and carry-out meals in polystyrene trays. The shops were closed or closing. The blustery wind made loose bits of litter blow against the shutters or skitter around his ankles. He didn't go far, just a few hundred yards to a pub, dodging through the traffic to cross the street. It was a tall building on the corner of a side street, all carved stone and strange-shaped windows leaking yellow light. Inside there were more pillars than people. The floor was bare wooden boards with oblong scraps of worn carpet that deadened the sound of two footsteps in the middle of his approach to the bar. He sat on a high stool and ordered a pint of Fuller's London Pride from a sullen barman with a ponytail and a ring through his nose. The other lone drinkers watched him curiously until he had raised the glass to his lips and taken a sip, then they went back to contemplating their own personal sadnesses.

It had been a very boring first day on the hostage negotiating course, much taken up with drinking coffee and instantly forgotten introductions to the thirty other DCI delegates from around the country. Then a couple of repetitive lectures on basic psychology interspersed with action clips from Hollywood films where the good guys always won. Nobody asked him about his personal experience of hostage taking, of standing on railings outside a house and shooting dead the man who was about to rape his wife. He knew the incident was recorded on his file and worried that he would be asked to discuss it. Then again why? There was no negotiation involved. A simple bullet through the window straight into the man's heart saved Sally and left the scene forever seared into his memory, framed by the jagged edges of the hole the bullet punched in the glass. No training course would have provided an alternative outcome to such a situation. Anyway, no one mentioned it and the long afternoon was rounded off with a promise of more interesting role-playing games the next day.

Fyfe shied away from the collective arrangements to meet for food and drinks that evening. He wanted to be alone. Back in his room he phoned home, talked banalities to Kate and Sally, then tried Hilary but there was no answer. He slept for a few hours and phoned in for an update on the dead girl in the cemetery, regarding the case as his personal property even though he had formally handed over responsibility. There was a definite shock of excitement, making the hairs on his neck stand on end, when

61

Matthewson told him that Belinda Struthers was the proud owner of an identical heart tattoo on her buttock, also dedicated to the unknown Bruce. She too was the victim of an identical but, as yet, unidentified poison. Belinda, it emerged, had been in social workers' care since the age of three when her mother overdosed on alcohol and no relatives would take her on. A succession of foster parents and children's homes followed until, as soon as she was sixteen, she exercised her right to adulthood and vanished through the holes in the welfare net to join the ranks of the undocumented underclass. The authorities had no further record of her until she was found propped up against the wall of a derelict house, deader than the bricks behind her. No friends had been uncovered. No leads at all. There had been no joy yet with local tattooists.

'We have to contact people of her own age she was in the children's homes with,' Fyfe told him.

'It's being done. Harper's on to it.'

Fyfe felt the distance between them wax hugely as he ended the call. His desire to be alone had been overwhelmed by a desire for a drink and the company of strangers. Harper was competent and sound, perfectly capable of handling the inquiry. He was one of the more independent-minded detectives, reminding Fyfe of himself sometimes. It was no good Fyfe trying to run the investigation by remote control from 400 miles away. There were already plenty of chiefs to control the Indians. He let it go, let it slip from his mind to be replaced by an image of Kate sitting beside him on the hillside with her head bowed, and Sally smiling invitingly at him as he got out of the car. And it was all mixed in with Hilary rising on tiptoe to kiss him farewell. Here's to Friday night, he thought eagerly and anxiously. He sighed, drank some beer, concentrated on the design of the grain on the wooden bar top and tried not to think at all.

'Worries, my friend?'

Fyfe looked up to see a man of roughly his own age with a badly bent nose and huge ear lobes. He was wearing a leather bomber jacket over a black tee-shirt. He had been through a windscreen at some stage in his life, leaving a myriad of tiny scars around his deep-set eyes and over his cheeks like tattoos on a Maori warrior. There was a blue tattoo of a spider's web on his throat. He had a rough but educated accent that hinted at unexpected intelligence. He didn't speak to the barman but a bottle of beer appeared in front of him. He picked it up by the neck with two fingers and swallowed half of it in a single action.

Fyfe didn't answer him. He bought himself another pint of London Pride and watched it settle in the glass to a clear brown liquid topped by a narrow white head. He drank some and its coldness created the sensory impression of an outline of his gullet leading down to his stomach, like a tactile x-ray picture.

'We all have worries, my friend,' the stranger continued, looking straight ahead. 'Some have more than others. That's the only difference.'

Fyfe felt a strong compulsion to engage in conversation rising through him like the bubbles on the beer. He resisted it, afraid that it might lead him in a direction he didn't want to go. Yet there seemed so much latent purpose in this chance meeting, almost as if it had been arranged so that he could unburden himself to this complete stranger and then walk away. He could tell any story he wanted, invention or the truth. No one would know. What harm could it do? But still Fyfe didn't say anything. He chewed the inside of his lip and drank more cold beer. The barman was quietly efficient. He read the small nod of Fyfe's head and filled the empty pint glass again.

'It's my children I worry about mostly,' the stranger said. 'My girl's had to give up her job because she's going to have a baby. I'm going to be a grandfather and all I can do is worry about the future for them.'

'Yeah,' Fyfe grunted, unable to hold back. 'I'm going to be a grandfather too.'

The stranger turned his head, encouraged by the response. 'Straight-up? Then why are we so gloomy? It's a wonderful life really.'

'Like you said, we worry about the future.'

'That must be it. When is yours due?'

'Months yet.'

'I've only got a few weeks to go,' the stranger confided. 'I suppose it could be any time now. Of course, her boyfriend claimed he couldn't handle the pregnancy thing. I had to sort him out.'

'You did?' Curiosity tugged like a sharp hook at Fyfe. Okay,

Doug wasn't the father but he needed sorting out anyway. 'How did you do that?'

'Bastard had kicked her out, told her it was all her own fault and she could look after herself. I went round and made him see sense. Now he admits he has a duty to support his kid. I can't afford it. I've got another two daughters coming up, prettier and dumber and more likely to fall pregnant. Couldn't let a trend be set, could I? Everyone is going to live happily ever after now. That's the theory anyway.'

'How did you do it?' Fyfe repeated.

'Do what?'

'Make him see sense?'

'I threatened to break his legs.'

'And did you?'

'No. The threat was enough. I have a certain reputation, you see.'

'Ah.' Fyfe almost admired the stranger's malevolent smirk. 'So did you have to break anything?'

'Only his front door to get at him. Oh, and his front teeth.'

They laughed and touched pint glass to beer bottle. Fyfe called in a round of beer and added whiskies. A rapport had been established although no names had been exchanged. With a long sigh of satisfaction, Fyfe began to picture the kneecapping of a suddenly repentant Doug. That would put a smile on Sally's face and it would teach the bastard to mess around with his only daughter. He had saved Sally, hadn't he? Shot dead the bastard who was threatening her. Why shouldn't he do the equivalent for his daughter? She deserved it, didn't she?

'It can't be a very sound basis for a happy family,' Fyfe said.

'Sound enough, believe me.'

'My son-in-law could do with a lesson in seeing sense.'

'Go and kick in his front door and teach him one then.'

'I couldn't do that. I'm a respectable citizen.'

'So am I. What do you do for a living?'

'Business. I'm a consultant.'

The lie came out as smoothly as the beer was going down. They had moved to a table by a head-high window. Late evening sun and the sodium street lights were filtering through a layer of dirt on the glass, making the spots and specks float translucently like specimens on a laboratory slide. The atmosphere was thick and oppressive. The combination of quickly absorbed alcohol and lack of food made Fyfe light-headed. He had entered an alternative lifestyle, a different world with different rules. He looked around and the other people in the pub had taken on a variety of sinister and curious profiles. They were the kind of pond life that lives under stones in scummy water and are seen only fleetingly as they move from one dark and dank hiding place to another. They were an amalgam of pointed jaws, rounded shoulders, hooked noses, bad skin conditions, dirty fingernails and bulging eyes. A ceiling fan rotated constantly, stirring up the waters, making people drift along in slowly moving currents of air. Fyfe felt at ease. Here in the pub, in the company of these strangers, he was no longer a respectable middle-class parent bound by normal civilized conventions. He felt himself changing, taking on a new identity that recognized the laws of nature rather than the laws of man. He was the father of a wronged daughter and he was thinking that his duty was to seek revenge for what had happened to her. The natural law said he should kill the bastard, or at least do him some damage.

'What do you do?' Fyfe asked the stranger opposite him.

'I've got a small building firm.'

'You said you had a reputation?'

'I did.'

'What for?'

'For not allowing myself to be fucked around.'

'I'd like a reputation like that.'

'It's yours, my friend. There for the taking.'

'I'd like to teach my son-in-law a lesson.'

'Need any help?'

'What have you got?'

'Experience.'

The conversation was now being conducted in whispers. Fyfe hunched over the table while the stranger sat back. He had a muscular body-builder's frame, probably produced by the weights in a prison gym, Fyfe thought. He recognized a professional criminal, a man accustomed to using violence as an everyday tool of his trade. To take him on and go ahead with a crazy plan dreamed up during a chance meeting in an anonymous pub would be the behavioural equivalent of a one-night stand with a willing and able woman. What the hell, Fyfe decided spontaneously, adultery could be fun and there was no need for a long-term commitment. Just get it over and done with and move on.

'He doesn't live far from here,' Fyfe said.

'That's handy.'

'What would you want in return?'

The stranger shrugged, emptied his whisky glass and beckoned to the barman for more. His eyes were slightly glazed, his lips glossy with saliva. 'Whatever.'

'You'd help me do it? I could pay you.'

Fyfe was aware of how artless he sounded, but the prospect of gaining revenge on Doug for the pain he had caused Kate was overwhelming. It was like an addiction that had to be satisfied, by whatever means. Fyfe repeated his question.

'Sure,' the stranger said, slurring his words very slightly. 'What are friends for? When do you want to do it?'

Fyfe remembered Sally's final words to him in the car at the airport. Why don't you kick the shit out of the little bastard. Of course, no responsible person would expect him to take the words seriously. But responsibility could mean different things to different people. A cold rage spread through Fyfe's body, reaching every extremity. He looked at his watch and when he spoke he barely recognized his voice.

'No time like the present,' he said.

19

Tuesday: 18.57

Connor Harper finished the half bottle of whisky, wrapped it in a tabloid newspaper and slipped it into the recycling waste bin, the only one with a lid. The incident room at police headquarters was almost empty of people now, except for him and DS Matthewson who kept disappearing to the toilet for some reason. The bulk of the nightshift were out doing a door-to-door on the latest development in the case. Doing it late at night meant most people were in. Harper knew he should go home but had no one to go home to. That afternoon he had visited his teenage children and handed over their presents. It had been going fine until ex-wife Anne started on at him about money and he made more promises he was never going to keep.

Harper wiped his nose, concentrating his attention as best he could. There were three bodies now. Another photograph was pinned to the big board above the map of the city with coloured flags showing the locations, one in the west, two within a mile of each other on the east side. It was a black and white blow up of a happy family snap, contrasting with the closed-eyes death masks of the two girls that had been taken in the mortuary. And there was no picture of the latest victim's buttocks because he had no tattoo. His name was Scott, not Bruce. The only connection was the same unidentified poison in his blood.

Harper bumped into the edge of a table and had to steady himself. He was tired and needed to get some sleep but didn't want to be on his own. He looked round the empty room with the glowing lights of the city beyond the windows and appreciated the irony. He put the last of his extra-strength mints in his mouth and the screwed-up packet followed the bottle into the bin. He turned to Scott Anderson's picture and tried once more to imagine what wondrous, reality-busting hallucination had taken over his mind when he jumped from the hospital window. It was an elegant movement, the nurse who tried to stop him had said. Graceful even. It was a strange description for such a self-destructive act. She was in shock, of course.

The inquiry had been ticking over nicely until Scott Anderson collapsed in the casualty department while being treated for a minor dog bite and brought himself to their attention because of what was in his blood. It was a logistical pity because the trawl of tattoo shops had found the skin artist who remembered his handiwork and whose records put a name to Belinda Struthers's pal, Virginia Stevenson. Both were Barnardo's girls who had run the full gauntlet of social services until they were sixteen and able to shake off the nanny state and vanish into a nether world, finally turning up dead a few years later. No dog bites on their bodies or that would have made it simple. As it was, the mongrel had dropped dead and a post-mortem on it was scheduled for the morning. Chances were its blood would have the same poison. But what did that mean?

This Scott Anderson had been, by all accounts, a happily married man. No criminal record except an unpaid parking ticket from two weeks previously, no history of mental illness, no dodgy connections, no nothing. He had been a weekend sailor and member of the local golf club. His wife was equally respectable, a teacher of flower arranging at night classes apparently. So maybe Scott led a secret life, calling himself Bruce and acting as pimp for teenage flotsam gathered from the streets. Maybe he picked up the young girls himself and indulged in wild orgies while his unsuspecting wife was out arranging flowers. Maybe he tried to make them have sex with his dog which just happened to be suffering from some mysterious blood disease. The dog went along with it, but when Scott tried to join in, he got himself bitten because the dog was a conscientious objector when it came to homosexuality. The girls then drop dead, so does the poor dog, and Scott panics and finally kills himself to avoid the shame. Well, it was a theory that fitted what facts they had so far. Not one he would care to put down in an official report, however.

'Excuse me, sir,' Matthewson said.

'Yes,' Harper replied, glad of the interruption although he hadn't noticed Matthewson coming back into the room.

'Message from Dr Thomson, sir.'

'The pathologist?'

'The same. Remember the maniac bus driver who killed himself today?'

'No. Vaguely, I suppose. I heard about it.'

'Well, a routine test for alcohol in his blood turned up an unknown substance. Further checks were made.'

Harper completed the sentence. 'And it turned out to be our poison.'

'It did. William Stoddart, resident of the same street as one Scott Anderson, also deceased.'

Harper whistled to show his surprise. 'What the fuck's going on out there. Is it something in the air or what? I don't suppose he had a tattoo on his backside?'

'There's more, sir. A message from the Met.'

'What do you mean? A weather forecast?'

'The Metropolitan Police, sir. In London.'

'What do they want?'

'They've got a victim, sir.'

'A victim? What kind of victim?'

'Some bloke with the same kind of poison in his blood as our ones. Same as the girls, same as Anderson, same as the bus driver. He was found on a cross-border train at King's Cross yesterday. It was noticed when a computer inquiry came in to the National Poisons Register from the hospital down in London.'

'The train from Edinburgh?'

Matthewson nodded. 'His name is Bruce, sir. Bruce Davidson.'

'Well, what do you know? Bruce of the backside. It must be him.'

'Could be.'

'So now we have five bodies.'

'Still four, sir,' Matthewson corrected. 'This one's not dead. He's unconscious in hospital but not dead.'

Harper smiled, accepting the credit for a breakthrough, if it was a breakthrough, which had come looking for him of its own accord. There had to be some connection between all the poison victims. It might take time but it would be found.

'We'd better tell them to keep the windows locked before he takes a header out of one then. We'll need to send somebody to check on this one.'

'DCI Fyfe is in London at the moment.'

'So he is. How convenient. He'll probably be grateful if we can give him an excuse to dodge that daft training course he's been sent on. We can get him involved in some real police work. He'll thank us for that, I'm sure.'

20

Tuesday: 23.10

This was wrong, very wrong. Fyfe squirmed in the back of the car, uncomfortable under the coarse woollen balaclava that smelled of washing powder and made his own warm breath slide over his cheeks like a greasy liquid. He had stepped outside the law before but it had never been premeditated. Always, it had been passive. A reaction to circumstances, not a deliberate, considered act of violence like this. He was a senior policeman for God's sake, his whole identity wrapped up in the rule of law. What was he doing in the company of a pair of pantomime villains about to inflict grievous bodily harm on an innocent man? And yet, even as his conscience struggled to control him by the normal common-sense arguments, there was a quieter part of him deep inside that had accepted the inevitability of and need for what was about to happen. It was, he told himself, right and proper. It was natural justice in the truest sense. Sally hadn't been joking when she said he should kick the shit out of the bastard who had hurt their precious daughter. She had been challenging him to do it. Besides, he thought, wishing to have it both ways, he hadn't initiated anything. It had come to him. The stranger had been waiting for him in the pub. What was for you, his mother had told him more than once, wouldn't go past you. Underneath the mask, looking out on a world restricted to a binocular-shaped field of vision, Fyfe smiled drunkenly and went with the flow.

It was going to be a Swiss cheese night, his memory of it already full of holes. The substance of it was the stranger sitting opposite him at the pub table as they plotted the attack, and then waiting outside on the pavement for the stranger's nephew to arrive in a soft-top Ford Escort, and then sitting in the back seat with Bruce Springsteen blaring out and instructions on what they were going to do being whispered into his ear. He was handed the balaclava mask and the sawn-off scaffolding pole that was to be used as a club. He was shown the canvas bag that was going to go over the victim's head and the whole procedure was explained to him in simple terms as if he was a customer at a garden centre being told how to deal with a nasty garden pest. It occurred to Fyfe during the explanation that he could prevent things going any further by refusing to say what Doug's address was, or by pretending not to remember it, or by giving the wrong one so that they would never find him. It was the last escape route for him, but it was shut off when he realized that the car had drawn up outside the house. He couldn't remember giving the address.

'Take the mask off,' the first stranger told him. 'Until we reach the door. No talking once we're inside. That's important.'

The street of identical terraced houses was deserted. Every second lamppost was out and there were only a few windows with lights on behind them. Clumps of cars lined the edge of both sides of the road. The stranger's nephew double parked, turned down the music and left the engine running. It was beautifully tuned, hardly made any noise. He lit a cigarette, looked back over his shoulder and grinned, showing a mouthful of uneven yellow teeth.

Fyfe followed the stranger up the short path where he and Sally had once walked to be met at the door by Kate, all smiles and nervous energy and apologies for Doug being late home from work. What had the real reason been? And when he did arrive he was withdrawn and distant, but Fyfe hadn't thought much about it, assuming it was because Doug was tired after his work or that the coolness was the result of the kind of temporary domestic dispute that was common enough, didn't he know it, for every married couple. And when they left, Kate had kissed him on the cheek and squeezed his hand, and he had walked away and left her to the mercy of her sadistic partner. He wondered if the bastard had started hitting her as soon as they had gone. The rage swelled inside him. He tightened his grip on the heavy scaffolding pole and banged it against his thigh as he waited.

The stranger was ringing the bell, pulling on his mask. Fyfe copied him, adjusting the eye-holes, feeling his face once more massaged by his warm breath. There was movement inside. A light went on. Footsteps. A muted voice, hoarse with sleep, asking who was there.

'It's the police,' the stranger said and Fyfe almost laughed out loud. 'It's about your wife, sir. I'm afraid there's been an accident.'

There was the sound of a key opening a lock and a chain being freed. The door had only moved back a few inches when the stranger hit it with his shoulder. Inside, Doug was knocked backwards along the hall and the stranger was on him in a flash,

71

pulling the canvas bag over his head with a sweeping motion and jerking the cord tight round his neck so that he coughed and choked. Doug, wearing only a dressing gown and boxer shorts, writhed helplessly but was trapped by the stranger sitting on his head, the palms of his hands held open towards Fyfe in a gesture of offering.

Fyfe hesitated but only for a moment. Then the vivid memory of Kate's badly bruised face and the pitiful tears leaking out of her blackened eyes enraged him. The terrible rush of anger was an elemental force, purging the alcohol from his system and triggering him into action. He kicked Doug in the side, raised the club high above his head and brought it crashing down on the naked knee joint. The dull thump of contact between steel and bone mingled with the muffled scream of pain. The legs tried to jerk away but there was nowhere for them to go. Twice more Fyfe slammed the club down with all the force he could muster. With the third blow there was the distinct sound of bone breaking. At the same time the screaming had changed to a low animal moaning. The stranger pointed urgently at the chest, leaning back to give free access. Fyfe's breath came in rapid gasps. He looked down on the naked flesh with the ribs pressing up through it. A flashback of Kate as a little child came to him. She was running down a hillside, her hair streaming in a warm breeze and he was snatching her up to swing her round. The idyllic scene shattered with the cracking thud of the club he brought crashing down on the exposed ribs and the arm beside them. Three times Fyfe hit out and then, abruptly, he was totally drained. All his anger seemed to have dissipated in the concentrated outburst of violence. He hardly had the strength to hold onto the piece of metal in his hand. A sense of unreality made him blink and shake his head. He thought he was being smothered and rolled the mask up over his mouth and nose to gulp in air.

The stranger stood up and pushed him out of the door. He turned and tore off the canvas bag. Doug lay where he was, curling up slowly as if he was going back to sleep. Fyfe went out into the quiet, still empty street, hurrying without running towards the parked car and the tempting security of the rear seat. The stranger was right behind him, patting him on the back, telling him it was a job well done. The stranger's nephew grinned from the driver's seat. Fyfe dropped the piece of scaffolding pole on the floor of the car and it rolled under the front seat. He threw the woollen mask down after it. He felt a strange sensation of calmness overcome him. He was drunk again, the alcohol was swamping his brain. He tried to communicate with Sally by telepathy to tell her what he had done. He imagined her lying in their bed with her eyes open, staring at the ceiling. When he imagined her smiling he knew he had got through to her.

In the car the stranger had taken the front passenger seat. He turned his head. 'Happy now?' he asked.

Fyfe considered the question seriously. He searched his conscience and listened again to the sound of sobbing and breaking bones. The car turned a corner, tilting him against the window, pressing the side of his cheek against the cold glass.

'I'm happy,' he admitted.

21

Wednesday: 00.24

The tenement landing was a cold and lonely place. The stairwell had been recently repaired and restored and was ready to be painted. Patches of new plasterwork dotted the walls. The big skylight in the roof was divided into three panes, one of which was brand new. Connor Harper was wearing a black army-style woollen hat pulled down over his ears, gloves and a rough tweed overcoat. He held a bunch of flowers, bought at a petrol station, behind his back. His feet in thin socks and ordinary shoes were the coldest part of his body. He shuffled them to prevent the cold from the stone floor penetrating upwards and looked around him, observing the smallest detail of his familiar surroundings. There was a huge spider's web in a corner high above him and a chip in the doorframe at eye level right in front of him. After ten minutes of inaction he reached out and rang the

73

bell above the nameplate that showed the flat belonged to Kelly Miller.

The door opened and a wave of dry heat emerged. An oblong of yellow light fell around Harper. Kelly stood in the doorway in a big tee-shirt outside jogging trousers, blonde hair piled loosely on top of her head. Her feet were overwhelmed by pink bunny slippers with sad expressions and forward-leaning floppy ears, and she looked directly at Harper waiting for him to speak. He thought she looked ridiculously young, far too young for him. How had he ever got involved with her?

'Hello, darling,' he said. 'Remember me?'

'No,' she replied, folding her arms.

'I'm sorry, Kelly. I'm really sorry. I'm indescribably sorry. I've never been so sorry. I apologize unreservedly for my behaviour. It was completely out of order. I'm sorry I spoiled our holiday. It was all my fault. No blame attaches to you whatsoever. What can I do to make it up to you?'

Harper thrust the flowers at her and she moved instinctively to accept them. He thought he saw a faint smile begin to break out on her tanned face as she looked down into the bunch. He had first met her when investigating a housebreaking at this very flat. The mutual attraction was obvious from the start. He never did find the thief who had kicked in the door and taken her television and video but he came back with a bunch of flowers and a pleading expression that won her over. Their affair was a volatile one to say the least. It was not the first time he had stood at the door and humbled himself in their personal version of sackcloth and ashes.

Kelly lifted her head and looked at him. She was definitely smiling now, definitely relenting, turning to one side to let him into the inner sanctum. There was much making up to do. Harper clapped his gloved hands together, shuffled his feet and prepared to step forward.

'Connor,' she said quietly.

'Darling?'

'Do me a favour.'

'Name it.'

Kelly hardly raised her voice at all. 'Fuck off, Connor.'

The floppy ears of the bunny slippers waved dramatically as

she twisted round to fling the flowers at him and slam the door in one unbroken movement. The heavy dead-locks he had advised her to buy and then installed for her clunked into position. Harper did not move. The flowers had hit him on the forehead and somehow balanced on his shoulder, falling individually to the ground from their clear plastic wrapping. He knelt down and picked them all up, holding the broken stalks in one hand and carefully laying them outside the closed door. More time was required to heal the breach between him and Kelly, it seemed. At least she hadn't hit him. The last bust-up had left him with a badly lacerated ear from trying to be too reasonable. Her fingernails were dangerous weapons.

He went down the stairs. There was a pub nearby that stayed open well past midnight. It was a place for people with lots on their mind. He could go there and contemplate the impenetrable riddle of the five poison victims, or he could try to understand women better. A solution to the first riddle seemed more promising. And going there meant he would have to spend less time on his own.

22

Wednesday: 10.53

Fyfe awoke in a cold sweat. He jerked upright in bed, instantly alert with a static tableau of the events of the previous night imprinted on his mind's eye and an empty feeling in his stomach that caused him to glance downwards to see if there was a hole there. It had been a dreamless sleep, ended by the persistent ringing of the phone which forced him to return to the real world.

'Jesus Christ,' he moaned. 'Jesus Christ. What have I done?'

His head was hurting and his mouth was dry, his lips sticking together. He was naked in the single bed under a single cotton sheet. The sun was burning through the thin curtain that covered the window in the tiny hotel room. He had no conception of what the time might be. All he could think of was the sickening sound of breaking bones and the physical injuries he had inflicted on the frantically squirming body with that heavy length of scaffolding pole. He held up his hand to examine it, still feeling the coarse texture of the steel against his flesh, moving his hand up and down to test the weight of the imaginary metal in his curled fingers.

Fyfe wanted it all to be a dream but knew that it was real enough. He had done it. He had stepped well outside the law and taken the chance to mete out his own brand of rough justice when the opportunity suddenly arose. It couldn't exactly be called spur of the moment when the whole episode had spanned several hours from his first encounter with the stranger in the pub through to the actual assault and then to him being dropped off several streets away so that they wouldn't know which hotel he was staying at. Throughout he had been rational, deliberate and self-aware. He had transgressed before, taking advantage of his position as a senior detective to help himself to a suitcase full of cash, but had justified it to himself as a victimless crime. No one was hurt, no one was any the wiser, so where was the harm in keeping a six-figure sum in used notes stashed under his garden shed while going about his daily business of catching thieves and robbers? He had long been a hypocrite. Now, it seemed, he had turned into a dangerously violent hypocrite.

How many times had he made the pompous speech to villains about how wrong it was to take the law into their own hands? How society couldn't function without proper respect for the law? How many times had he shaken his head at a petty villain's inability to comprehend the necessity for a strict code of law and order to prevent society's descent down a slippery slope into anarchy? This time he had gone too far, stepped so far over the line he could hardly see it behind him. Any court in the land would sympathize with him because of what had happened to his daughter, but any court would also convict him on a charge of assault leading to severe injury. There were no excuses for his behaviour, no shred of justification. And yet, he couldn't work up any feelings of guilt or shame for what he had done. He tried hard to conform to the conventional thinking that had been dinned into him as an upholder of the law, but failed. He realized that in fact, looking back, he was rather proud of himself for exposing himself to the risk. He had done it for his daughter Kate so that while her bruises faded, her worthless husband would be nursing bruises of his own. And, if he was honest, he had rather enjoyed it. Sally would approve too, so that made it all right. There was law and there was justice. Sometimes the two were incompatible. This was justice. It was all very well being sensible and civilized but sometimes it was better to bypass the clumsy limitations of human law and allow the laws of nature and blood to take precedence. An eye for an eye, a bruise for a bruise, a beating for a beating. Fyfe believed he had done well. He would have liked to describe the intimate details to Sally and Kate and be appreciated as the vengeful father risking all in defending his daughter's honour. He would have liked to tell Hilary so that she would know what a great guy he was and therefore invite him to sleep, as well as swim, with her. He would have liked to, but he was aware he would not do it because the rules he made up as he went along meant it had to remain his secret otherwise, somehow, the whole act would be devalued.

He would do it again, he decided, given the same circumstances and the same opportunity. His only regret was having to get revenge for Kate while in the company of strangers. If he was a religious man, he would have rationalized it by believing that they had been sent by God in one of his mysterious movements to help him out. He wasn't religious, but he was pragmatic, taking the chance when it presented itself. Another night and it would never have happened. Yet another and more reckless intervention could easily have resulted in Doug ending up dead.

The strangers had been the catalyst, of course, and therefore unavoidable but he just hoped he had maintained sufficient self-control not to let them know his name. He had been drunk and there were gaps in his memory, a long period in which he somehow found himself transferred from the dingy pub into the back seat of the Ford Escort with no apparent space in between. And there was another blank period just before he stepped out of the car after the deed was done. He could see the hieroglyphics of the orange sodium street lights reflected in the grease-streaked windscreen and all jumbled up with them the suddenly sinister faces of the obliging stranger and his grinning nephew leering back at him from the front seats while the scaffolding pole bumped against his feet on the floor of the car.

The phone had stopped ringing, drenching the room in a sticky silence. It must be another hot day outside, Fyfe thought. He shook his head and the movement carried on through his whole body like a dog shaking itself dry. He crawled off the bed and got a bottle of sparkling mineral water out of the mini-bar. The bubbles cured his thirst and settled his headache. He found his mobile phone and realized that the batteries were totally run down. He picked up his watch and cursed when he saw it was almost eleven o'clock. He had arranged to be at the lecture hall by ten. He didn't want to draw attention to himself by being any later than he could help, although that looked like a lost cause now. He would just have to play to the stereotype of the hard-drinking Scotsman out on a binge in the big city. They would understand that and accept it. Fyfe got an outside line and called the contact extension. It was answered on the second ring by Kevin Carruthers, the Scotland Yard liaison man in charge of running the training course. Fyfe had struck up an easy rapport with him and had almost accepted his invitation to go for a drink at the end of the first day, before inventing a fictitious friend who was waiting for him so that he could be alone to brood over Kate's situation. As things worked out, he hadn't remained alone for very long. If he had stayed with Carruthers he wouldn't have been late at all. Nothing would have happened.

'I tried to get you at the hotel a few moments ago,' Carruthers said. 'There was no answer from your room.'

'I'm down in the reception area,' Fyfe lied, beginning his damage limitation exercise. 'I've just had a late breakfast. I slept in, I'm afraid.'

'Hard night?'

'Harder than some.'

'No damage I hope.'

'Not to me anyway.'

'How are you?'

'A little delicate but I'll be with you soon. Can you cover for me?'

'You haven't got the message from your troops then?'

78

'What message?'

'They were looking for you last night. Some kind of emergency. They need you to go and interview somebody.'

'Who? Where?'

'I don't have any details but it looks like there's a villain down here in London they want you to ask some pertinent questions.'

Fyfe noticed an envelope that had been pushed under the door. Still with the phone to his ear he leaned over and picked it up. It had his name and room number written on it and the time of delivery, more than twelve hours previously. He must have walked right over it when he got back. The note inside told him to contact Connor Harper at the incident room as soon as possible regarding the girl in the cemetery.

'One of your guys I spoke to went on about a breakthrough in the girl in the cemetery case,' Carruthers said. 'He was on about finding Bruce. Backside Bruce he called him. Does that make sense to you?'

'Perfect sense. Looks like hostage negotiation will have to wait for another time.'

'Right then. I'll leave you to it. I'll write you off for today. Let me know the score later, if you're going to turn up tomorrow.'

Fyfe hung up and immediately got another line to phone Edinburgh. Pete Crichton answered and quickly explained the developments. On the back of the message envelope, Fyfe scribbled down the name of the hospital where Davidson was under observation and the local police station that was primed to give him any assistance he needed. Crichton finished by mentioning casually that Connor Harper had just walked in the door and looked like death warmed up. 'I know the feeling,' Fyfe said.

Inside Fyfe's head a new mind-set focusing on Bruce Davidson and the girl in the cemetery struggled to gain priority over the rabble of thoughts trying to pick holes in his mental conviction that there were no loose ends in last night's episode that could link him to the attack on Doug.

He got out of bed and set about finding the clothes he had been wearing. They were strewn haphazardly over the floor. He checked them for bloodstains but found none. He worried that there would be an abundance of forensic evidence left in Doug's house that could connect him with the attack, but he reasoned

79

that he could legitimately claim to have been in the house on previous occasions. Nobody was going to accuse him anyway. He was a DCI after all. Who in their right minds would believe that a person in his position would be capable of such a crazy thing? I ask you, ladies and gentlemen of the jury, is it reasonable?

Fyfe grinned, pleased by his own logic, and then frowned when he thought of the balaclava mask. It would be full of his hair, flakes of his skin. If it was sent to the appropriate place with an anonymous note explaining what had happened it could be damning. He couldn't remember what he had done with the balaclava. Had he left it in the car? No. He must have stuffed it in his pocket. He found it lying on the corner of the bed, drooping down like an icon in a Salvador Dali painting. He picked it up and pulled it on and looked at himself, still naked from the neck down, in the full-length mirror on the wall. He turned sideways and the sight of his single eye surrounded by the green wool reminded him of the moss around the eye of the stone angel embedded in the ground alongside the dead girl. Virginia Stevenson her name had been, and although the surname had been too badly eroded to read, he slowly remembered Virginia was the Christian name carved on the plinth of the grave the fallen angel had once stood sentry over.

Fyfe went to the window and drew back the curtains. Until The Day Breaks, he thought, as he opened his eyes wide and allowed himself to be dazzled by the bright sunshine. He needed to occupy his mind with current business. He needed to concentrate on Bruce Davidson. For the time being anyway.

23

Wednesday: 11.12

The screeching of the birds and the roars of the animals filled the jungle that surrounded Bruce Davidson on all sides. He crouched among the roots of one of the huge trees that towered over him, spreading their branches to create a green canopy that shut out light from above apart from self-contained thin lines that carved through the open space between the trees like a lattice-work of laser beams. He had seen the same kind of pattern made by the alarm systems in houses he had broken into. Break the beam, spoil the raid. Not here though. There were no houses here. He passed his hand through one of the beams of sunlight and saw the white circle it formed on the palm. The skin bubbled and burned. He could see it and smell it. He could hear the flesh sizzling. But he could not feel anything more than a slight tickling sensation. And when he moved his hand away the skin was restored to its former state within seconds. He moved his head so several of the beams fell on his face at once and he laughed as the skin began to pucker and pop and the strong scent of cooking human flesh filled his nostrils.

They had tried to hide his clothes but he had found them and quietly got dressed when he was left alone. It had been difficult because they did not leave him alone often. They kept asking questions and shining lights in his eyes, but he pretended he couldn't hear and just kept staring straight ahead and ignoring them. They shouted and a couple of times they punched his arm. He did not respond. They stuck pins in the soles of his feet and in his fingertips but it was easy for him to control the pain and ensure a negative reaction.

Now they were plotting outside the circle of trees that contained him. He had caught a glimpse of a huddle of silverback gorillas in the distance as they left. He realized that he would have to escape. Obviously, their plan was to use the silverbacks to terrify him into a reaction to prove he was faking it so they could kill him because he had fooled them for so long. He was frightened because the silverbacks were powerful, dangerous animals that could tear him limb from limb if they wanted to. Their weakness was that they were only trained to follow orders and would not have been ordered to kill him, because they would want that pleasure for themselves. Also, he had the element of surprise on his side. He had the choice of the first move. He was confident he would choose well and choose wisely when it came to the critical moment.

He was not afraid. He was not frightened of physical hurt.

81

What frightened him as he stood with his back against the coarse trunk of a giant tree was his inability to remember his past. He did not know how he came to be in the jungle, or why the people in black and silver were harassing him so intently. He knew some things, but not others. He knew about the trees, and the animals and birds. He knew that insects and frogs could kill, that sunlight burned skin, and that sharp needles drew blood. He knew how to tie his shoe laces and how to comb his hair flat with his fingers. He knew he was besieged by enemies. Yet he did not know why the water they gave him to drink was orange or why they should put a bed with white sheets and soft pillows out in the middle of the jungle. He did not know who he was or where he came from. There were vague memories in the back of his mind, but they were as indeterminate as the host of shapes that flitted continually among the trees around him. He suspected that he had been kidnapped by these people and therefore he must be somebody important and that it was his duty to escape so that he could return. Where should he return to? He would probably remember where in due course.

They were coming to get him now, the silverbacks. He could hear them approaching, the sound of their rushing steps growing louder and closer, shaking the ground around him. The waiting was over. The tree bark behind him was alternatively rough and solid or smooth and pliable to the touch of his hands. It was time to choose. He knew what he had to do. He was not afraid.

24

Wednesday: 12.15

David Fyfe took a taxi from his hotel to the police station and told the driver to go a few hundred yards beyond it along the road before paying him off and getting out. He wandered around the streets until he found what he was looking for, a builder's skip that was almost full of debris from a house that was being gutted. He checked that there was no one watching in the near-deserted street, then wrapped a half brick inside the balaclava mask and tossed it into a broken plastic barrel that already had a mixture of rainwater and oil slopping over its sides. Satisfied, he retraced his steps, found the police station and announced himself at the reception. A young black police-woman had been delegated to look after him and take him to the hospital to see Davidson. Her name was Joan and she was newly out of uniform and into a tight skirt and blouse, the old desk sergeant informed him, so be gentle with her. There was no one else available because the station was busy. Lots of crimes last night apparently, lots of investigations under way. Fyfe did not know what part of the city he was in, or whether he was any-where near Doug who, even now as he licked his wounds, could be explaining to a couple of detectives that he had no idea who might be responsible for the unprovoked attack on him.

Joan was bright and keen. In a back room she had Davidson's tatty holdall that had been found on the empty train at King's Cross and handed in to lost property before he was discovered in the toilet. It was matched to him by the contents of a zip-closing leather pouch that contained a membership card for a video shop in Edinburgh with his picture on it. Also in the pouch was a wallet of more than thirty photographs recently de-veloped at a Kwik Foto branch. Also in the holdall were some spare clothes, a pair of shoes, and two sixty-minute video cas-settes in their original boxes. One box had 'Lust for our An-cestors' written in ink on the spine, the other had 'The Homecoming'. Porn films almost certainly, Joan said. Something to keep the mind active on a quiet evening.

Fyfe opened the wallet of photographs and began to flick through them. The first couple were just bad pictures, out of focus and unrecognizable. The developer had stuck on paper labels recommending more light and higher shutter speeds. Then there were several featuring a fairly ordinary-looking man in his early twenties standing in front of some bushes or tree branches. In one he had a white bird sitting on his shoulder. Fyfe held it up for Joan to see.

'Davidson?' he asked.

'That's our boy,' she replied. 'Definitely.'

'Which one?'

'Not the parakeet.'

Fyfe nodded, returned the picture to the pack and continued shuffling through the remainder. Six from the end he suddenly stopped. He looked up at Joan and she raised her eyebrows and shrugged.

'We've no idea who it is,' she said in answer to the unspoken question.

'I do,' Fyfe said. 'It's the girl in the cemetery.'

He sat at a table and studied the photograph carefully. Davidson, or whoever had taken it, had got the light and shutter operation right. It was perfectly in focus, the colours were vivid, and every detail had been captured. The girl Fyfe now knew as Virginia Stevenson was standing in the overgrown graveyard and the sunlight was filtering down through the overhead branches creating a dappled pattern. She had on the jeans and the anorak and she was standing with one foot on the stone angel that had toppled from the plinth that bore her name. She was standing as a hunter stands over fallen prey, with her arms folded over her chest and her head tilted cheekily to one side. Her hair was all tangled in the wind and the expression on her face was designed to show what a clever girl she was. Behind her, just out of sight, was the space where Fyfe had seen her lying dead.

'Is she your murder victim?' Joan asked, lowering her head to his shoulder level, her voice lowered too in sympathy for the dead.

'She is.'

'And they found her in that cemetery?'

'That very one.'

'Oooo. It gives you the creeps, doesn't it? Walking on her own grave.'

There were two other photographs of Virginia, at least one of them taken in the graveyard. Then there was a close-up of another teenage girl, sticking her tongue out at the camera. Fyfe maybe wouldn't have recognized her in isolation but with the benefit of context he was sure she was Belinda Struthers. There was no identifiable background to the two pictures she appeared in, but a hunch told him she too was standing close to the spot where she ended up dead.

'And this is our other victim,' he said.

'Oooo. Is this bloke Davidson the prime suspect then?'

'Well, he's got a bit of explaining to do.'

'They were poisoned, weren't they?'

'So was Davidson.'

'A crime of passion,' Joan said, still whispering. 'A suicide pact. It's almost romantic, isn't it? Is it true both girls had identical tattoos on their bottoms?'

'Nobody is supposed to know that,' Fyfe said. 'But yes, it's true.'

'The bloke Davidson doesn't. Have a tattoo that is.'

'How do you know?'

She grinned hugely. 'I sneaked a look earlier when the nurses were washing him.'

Fyfe gathered the photos of the girls and slipped them into a separate plastic bag. He asked Joan to have copies made of them and rang the Edinburgh headquarters while she went to arrange it. When he couldn't get hold of Harper himself he decided not to pass on the information about the photographs until after he had seen Bruce Davidson. No point in telling half a story when he might have the whole story to relate.

Joan organized a lift for them to the hospital. On the way she explained how Davidson had refused to answer any questions at all when he recovered consciousness, just stared straight ahead. The doctors couldn't make up their minds if it was an act or a genuine psychological condition. It got boring trying to get anything out of him after a while, she said. Fyfe was welcome to him. Her bosses had plenty of their own criminals to be going on with.

The hospital was a large, outwardly featureless modern building with a confusing profusion of signs pointing in all directions to a dozen different departments. Joan knew where to go once they were dropped off beside casualty, straight up to the third floor. A policeman was sitting outside the door on a chair angled backwards onto two legs to rest against the wall. He had his hands on his knees and the toes of his shoes pointed like a ballet dancer. He jumped to attention in front of Fyfe and the chair rocked precariously but Joan steadied it before it fell over.

'Any problems, Constable?' Fyfe asked.

85

'None. He's quiet as a mouse in there.'

Fyfe looked through the window in the door. The bed was obscured by a partly drawn curtain. He opened the door and went inside. A slatted blind over the main window was not properly shut. It caused thin shafts of light, full of drifting dust particles, to dissect the room. Fyfe marched through the door confidently. He needed three steps to be able to see the bed clearly. In the same instant that he realized the bed was empty his field of vision became entirely filled by a looming figure he recognized from the photographs as Bruce Davidson. The grimacing face came hurtling towards him and vanished in co-ordination with the sound of a sudden loud thump.

'Oooo,' he heard Joan scream as he fell backwards, losing consciousness before he hit the floor.

25

Wednesday: 14.37

Joan hovered above, forming gradually in front of him like one of those pictures in television quiz shows where each feature is revealed separately before the final figure takes shape. He saw her hair hooked behind her ears to hang vertically down. There were tiny reflected stars in her eyes and a sheen on her cheeks. Her teeth shone whitely. The bones of her neck stood out under the skin that was stretched over the hollow of her throat. The desk sergeant had been right. Her blouse certainly was a bit tight.

'How are you feeling?' Joan asked.

Fyfe paid attention to the dull, thumping pain behind his eyes. Every few minutes it changed to become something very like a sharp chisel being driven into the bridge of his nose. The nose itself felt uncomfortably huge and very, very tender. When he moved a hand up to try and touch it to check that it was real, Joan caught his wrist to stop him. Her mouth grew larger, her teeth whiter, as she shook her head and smiled down encouragingly.

'I wouldn't do that,' she said. 'He head-butted you.'

'Who did?'

'Davidson. He ambushed us.'

Fyfe took a few seconds to identify Davidson. He examined Joan's nose, perfectly straight with delicately flared nostrils, and a slightly upturned tip. He tried to touch his own nose again but she held onto his wrist. The pain behind his eyes pulsed rhythmically and assumed a sharper edge with every third beat. Fyfe blinked and Joan's face reassembled itself above him more quickly this time. He remembered the previous night and Doug lying in the hallway curled up and moaning in pain after the beating he had received. Now it was his turn to do the moaning, a low mournful sound exhaled on every breath.

'He headed you something awful,' Joan informed him. 'You didn't have a chance. He came out from behind the curtain like a madman. It must be sore but at least it doesn't seem to be bleeding. It's probably broken.'

Still holding onto Fyfe's wrist, she reached out with her fingers and didn't quite touch his nose. The approaching fingertips became blurred smudges that caused a delayed reaction in Fyfe, making him jerk his head back and increase the intensity of the nagging pain. When he re-opened his eyes Joan's face was already there, in one nicely arranged piece. It would be rewarding, he thought, to go swimming with Joan.

'Are you all right?' he asked.

'He didn't touch me. After he hit you he just kept running right out the door. He was off like a rat up a drainpipe.'

'Let's get after him then.'

Fyfe struggled to get up but was easily held down. It was only then that Fyfe realized he was in a hospital bed wearing a surgical gown and that, as well as Joan, there were two doctors and a nurse standing round him. He relaxed and closed his eyes. The pain pulsed quietly inside his skull.

'There's no point,' Joan said. 'He's long gone from here.'

'How long have I been out?'

'About two hours, maybe a little longer.'

Fyfe tried to rationalize the information. Two hours had vanished from his life. The memory of Davidson's face looming in front of him was now very vivid. Then it was replaced by Joan's white teeth. In between there was the thinnest of lines, but it turned out to be two hours, maybe more, wide. A lot could happen in two hours, he thought. When he had been lying unconscious they could have tattooed his backside. Another of Bruce Davidson's poor victims. He clenched his buttocks and felt nothing out of the ordinary.

'No need to hurry then, if he's gone,' Fyfe said.

'We'll find him,' Joan said. 'We've got a description circulating now.'

'When we find him will you do me a favour, Joan?'

'Of course. What do you want? Name it.'

'You go in first.'

26

Wednesday: 18.23

The girl had been found just before midnight in an anarchic squat on the edge of the Georgian architectural splendour of Edinburgh's New Town. It was all torn carpets, overflowing ashtrays, and heavy metal music posters. Her name was Sarah Smith and she approached the officers who were being mostly sneered at or ignored by everyone else. She had read about the killings in the papers and wanted to help, she said. She had been a friend of both Virginia Stevenson and Belinda Struthers, had been in the same children's homes, had known them all her life, or at least as much of it as she could remember. She would appreciate a good meal because afterwards she was sure she would be able to tell them everything they wanted to know. She got the meal and a bundle of old clothes that had accumulated in the locker room at police headquarters. Everybody felt sorry for her so they had a whip round and raised thirty pounds.

'Go on then, Sarah,' Connor Harper said, switching on the tape to record the interview. 'Tell us about your friends.'

Sarah's story was almost certainly true. Harper only had to look into her dull, opaque eyes to see that she was incapable of invention from her own imagination. Three girls on their own, not entitled to any benefits because of their age and mostly unemployable except for short-term jobs as waitresses or barmaids, and submerged in a hopeless, drug-saturated nether world. Sarah was quite candid about their drug-taking, paid for largely by prostitution and theft. She had done nothing wrong. She had done what she had to do to survive, she told him defiantly. Harper didn't argue with her. She was tiny, painfully thin with lifeless hair, sunken cheeks and a pointed chin. If she had put some weight on and cleaned herself up she might have been attractive, but she wasn't. She had a waif-like charm from a distance that disappeared on closer examination. She didn't have an answer for why she hadn't offered to help before she was found. She didn't seem to understand the question. All the time, she sat clutching a mug of hot tea in both hands, watching the steam rising from it in apparent fascination, like a medium trying to contact the other side.

'Bruce Davidson, the bastard.' She turned her head to one side and pretended to spit on the floor. 'I didn't like him. He was bad news. I could smell him a mile off but Ginny and Belinda were taken in. He would look after them, he said. He would see they were all right, all fine and dandy. Come with me and the world will be perfect. The stupid bitches fell for it. He was just a pimp, another pimp, that was all. He only wanted them so he could use them for his own purposes. Bruce Davidson was a bastard and a half. He was twisted, too. If I had listened to him I would be dead now.'

Harper didn't change his opinion of Sarah. He felt sorry for her, a quid's worth of sorrow. Dumb animals could pick out the bad bastards in the human race, it was a sixth sense they had. But it didn't stop them being dumb animals.

'How do you mean twisted?' Harper asked.

'Twisted. You know. A pervert. He got his kicks from watching not from doing.'

'How do you know?'

'I know. He was into dirty films, holes drilled in wardrobes, hidden cameras.'

'Blackmail?'

'Probably. As soon as I heard Ginny's body had been found in that graveyard I knew who had done it.'

'Did you now?'

'Yeah. It was Ginny's favourite place, you see. That's why that twisted bastard put her there.'

'The graveyard was her favourite place?'

'Yes.'

'Bit gloomy, isn't it?'

'Depends. And then Bel was found right beside where she was born. She always used to talk about where she was born, said her life would have been so different if her mother hadn't died. It's just like Davidson to make her die there. He'd think that was funny.'

'Why was Ginny's favourite place a graveyard?'

'Because of the headstone.'

'What headstone?'

'The one right in the centre, the angel that's fallen on its face. It has her name carved on it. Virginia Stevenson, the exact same name as Ginny, but she died one hundred years earlier. We used to sit there a lot and try to imagine what she must have been like, the hundred-year-old dead girl I mean. Ginny used to say that she was probably her reincarnation.'

Harper recalled the layout of the cemetery and the fallen statue of the angel with the human body lying alongside it, mimicking its position. He thought of Kelly in her floppy bunny slippers and he wondered if Fyfe would recover quickly from the attack by this nutcase Davidson. If it had been him, Harper, on the receiving end, he would have milked the injury for as much time off as possible. Headaches, unable to sleep, stress, that kind of stuff.

'Then there was Bel as well. He put her right in the street where she was born. What a bastard. That's what I mean by twisted.'

'Bel?' Harper concentrated on what was being said to him. 'You mean Belinda?'

'Yeah.'

'Davidson a local guy?'

'No. He's English. Makes him even more of a bastard.'

'Do you know anybody called Scott Anderson?'

'No.'

'Or Billy Stoddart?'

'No.'

'You might know them by different names. Look at these photographs.'

Sarah studied the photos carefully and repeated her denial. Harper believed her. She wasn't a good enough actress to be able to lie convincingly. The Davidson connection with the two girls was plain, but where did that leave the near neighbours Anderson and Stoddart and the rabid dog. There had to be a link somewhere. They had all died from the same mysterious poison that the experts couldn't identify. Harper had been out to the houses, unremarkable, terraced, nothing to be found in either of them, except one grieving and bewildered widow. She said they never spoke to Stoddart, never saw him. He was a bus driver, living on his own, heavily into carry-out meals and carry-out drink. Scott was an insurance salesman, she worked as a secretary in a lawyer's office. They had absolutely no contact, she insisted. Except both men had died of the same poison. Harper had stood outside the houses at the rear, watching the rows of shoulder-to-shoulder officers fingertip search the gardens. Nothing was found. He took a deep breath and wondered seriously if it was something in the air.

'Do you know anyone with a dog, Sarah?'

'Lots of people.'

'A dog called Rex.'

'Maybe.'

Harper sighed and tried a different tack. 'Do you know where Davidson lived?'

'Maybe.'

'Do you or don't you?'

'Yes.'

'Where is it?'

'Don't know the name but I could show you.'

'Let's go then.'

Crichton drove the car with Munro in the passenger seat. Harper sat in the back with Sarah, who curled up silently in the corner and stared out of the window. Davidson had a rented flat in a flat-roofed block of six in one of the rougher housing schemes in the north of the city. The ground-floor windows of the block were boarded up and the entrance to the stairs had an iron gate held by a broken padlock. On the first floor someone had thrown a tin of green and then a tin of yellow paint over the wall and Davidson's door as pointed out by Sarah. It looked like something that should have been in a modern art gallery. The paint job had happened after the door had been repaired. A piece of paper taped to the surface and partially covered in paint said that the electricity had been cut off only three days ago.

'No answer,' said Harper after knocking. 'What a surprise. What do we do now? Go and get a search warrant.'

'Hot pursuit of a suspect, sir,' said Crichton.

'Very hot, since we know he's on the run down in London after assaulting a police officer. I don't think we can get any hotter. Stuff the warrant, let's kick it in.'

Crichton went first, standing back and kicking with the sole of his foot at the area just below the handle. Munro copied him and they began to work to a proper rhythm, like precisely choreographed dancers. The door had been repaired well by the electricity company. It gave way only gradually, tottering like a defenceless boxer trying to stand his ground. When it finally broke and swung open a six-foot tall splinter came away from the frame.

The flat was empty. In the kitchen a loaf of bread was stale and as solid as a brick. There was mould on the cheese in the fridge and a thick scum on the water piled with dirty dishes in the sink. The bedroom had one double bed and a mattress on the floor, nothing else. The living room had a carpet, a threadbare settee and a couple of shaky-looking chairs. The big expensive wide-screen television in the corner looked totally out of place in the poverty of its surroundings. In the cabinet beneath it was a row of more than two dozen video cassette boxes.

'At least he left us something to watch,' Harper said. 'Think your friends will be in any of these, Sarah?'

He looked back over his shoulder but Sarah was gone. Harper hurried down the stairs to the entrance but she had vanished with her bundle of second-hand clothes and her pocketful of money, swallowed up by the night and the city. They would hunt for her again, Harper knew, but the odds were against finding her. There were too many places to hide. She was gone.

27

David Fyfe caught the last shuttle flight north from Heathrow. The hospital had wanted to keep him in overnight but he insisted on being discharged, telling the doctor that there was no place like home for convalescence. He had decided that there was no point in him staying while the local police hunted for Davidson, or to restart the hostage negotiation course with only one day left. Joan collected his stuff from the hotel and delivered it to him along with the rest of Davidson's possessions. He wanted to, but didn't, ask her if there were any reports of apparently random attacks on people at their front doors. Joan drove him out to the airport, shook hands, wished him well and left him alone.

Inside the terminal he bought a pair of dark glasses to hide the light bruising that encircled his eyes. His nose was tender to the touch but, although it felt hugely swollen, was not particularly big when he saw it in the mirror. There was a vertical cut on the bridge but it had quickly healed. His nose looked bent, but only slightly, to the right. Behind the bruises he didn't look too bad. He looked faintly ridiculous, like a lemur or somebody who had applied mascara very badly. But he also looked like a victim in need of sympathy and he knew exactly where to get it. He phoned home and gave Sally an edited version of what had happened to him at the hospital. He spoke briefly to Kate as well and told them both not to worry, that he would be back in the morning. They didn't sound too concerned. He tried to get hold of Connor Harper but had no luck. An update on the murder investigation from an anonymous officer failed to make much impression because his mind wasn't on it. They had already linked the dead girls and Bruce Davidson so his photographs were no great revelation. He phoned Hilary from the same public phone as the faceless crowds milled around him.

'What kind of welcome would I get if I turned up at your door tonight with a bottle of good wine?' he asked.

'A very warm welcome indeed,' she replied.

He took a taxi straight from Edinburgh airport to her door, stopping off on the way to buy the wine he had promised. She answered the door almost as soon as he pressed the bell and was about to kiss him in greeting when he instinctively jerked his head back. She hesitated and frowned uncertainly. He took the glasses off and, within seconds, saw the sympathy kick in. Hilary took his bag and escorted him, invalid-style, upstairs to the living room. He told her his story about the attempted interview with the murder inquiry suspect ending abruptly before it had begun. She got a damp cloth and gently dabbed at the bruises round his eyes, making sympathetic noises. He flinched a couple of times although she wasn't hurting him at all.

'You know, Dave, there is something I've never done,' she said.

'Really?'

'Yes.'

'Would you like to do it now?'

'I think I would.'

'What is it then?'

'I've never made love to somebody who has two black eyes.'

That was it. They were in her bedroom, throwing off their clothes as they went, and naked under the sheets within two minutes. Their impatient love-making and desperate mouth-to-mouth kissing lasted the same amount of time and they lay for ages with arms and legs wrapped tightly around one another. Hilary kept arching her back and pushing herself against him with surprising strength, searching for his mouth to kiss him again and again. Kissing caused Fyfe pain across the bridge of his battered nose but he didn't admit to it in case she stopped. He suffered it and when he moaned she took it for encouragement. Eventually, they lay bundled together in exhausted silence. He realized then that the room was surprisingly small, with little floor space around the big double bed itself, but an entire wall of mirror doors gave the illusion of it being much bigger.

'Can you stay?' she asked in a voice so small he could hardly hear her.

'Yes,' he answered.

Hilary relaxed then and, still draped around him, fell asleep almost instantly. Fyfe felt her grip on him slowly slacken. He listened to her breathing become as regular as the heartbeat that ticked softly against his rib cage. He was wide awake, looking around the unfamiliar room with curiosity while trying to judge the full significance of what he and Hilary had just set in motion. The bond that they had forged in a few minutes of physical urgency was, he suspected, not just another random and unconnected episode in his life but something important and influential that would have consequences he could not yet imagine. It was not that he intended to abandon Sally again and move in with Hilary. It wasn't just the sex. The sense of impending disaster went much deeper, although what form the disaster would take was vague and shapeless in his mind. It seemed to be a sense that he had somehow crossed another line by making love to Hilary and no matter what he did from here on in, he would always be on the wrong side of that line and could not deny it, at least not to himself. It had been the same the previous night with the stranger in the pub and the attack on his son-in-law Doug. He had no regrets about that either. It had needed doing. But Fyfe was storing up trouble for himself. When the reckoning arrived to haunt him, he would have to hold up his hands and admit to being the author of his own misfortune.

Fyfe squeezed the back of Hilary's neck with one hand and rubbed the thigh that lay over his stomach with the other. Her warm breath spilled over his chest. He luxuriated in the radiating heat from her body. He had no regrets. He would do it all over again, hoped to have the chance soon. He would deal with the consequences when they came, whatever they were. He would cope. It was the way he survived from day to day. It was the only way to stay sane.

After twenty minutes he disentangled himself from Hilary and slid out of the bed. The relatively cold air was pleasantly cool against his bare skin, flowing over him as he felt his way along the walls in the darkened hallway to the living room. Two empty crystal glasses and the unopened bottle of wine were standing on the table beside a shaded lamp that cast a soft light at low level. The corkscrew was nearby, its limbs splayed outwards in an animated parody of a stainless-steel murder victim, and next to it was his useless mobile phone. He took the charging unit from his coat, which was lying on the floor, and plugged one end into the flat battery and the other into a power point in the skirting boards. Fyfe looked down on the glowing red light that would soon connect him to the outside world as he used the corkscrew to open the bottle. The cork squealed a little as it gave, coming out with a hollow pop that seemed unnaturally loud in the quietness of the room. He poured a glass and carried it over to the window, moving the curtains aside carefully to look out without making himself visible.

Moonlight reflected from the dark tarmac of the road, and the tiles on the roofs of the houses opposite. The nearest street lamp swayed in the wind, smudging the rectangular blob of its yellow sodium light that was flecked by the occasional raindrop. All the windows facing him were dark, doors were firmly closed. Cars with blank windscreens were parked at irregular intervals along both sides of the street. Fyfe thought he saw a movement. It was just a momentary flicker, impossible to identify, like the wings of a bird flapping amongst the skeletal branches of a winter tree, but it caught his attention, tensing his whole body and stopping the wine glass a few inches from his mouth. He replayed the movement in his head, assigning it imagined detail, seeing a face, shoulders, a head ducking out of sight behind one of the cars. He stared intently at the spot where he thought he had seen it. He stared until the pain at the bridge of his nose was accentuated by snail trails of dead cells slithering over his eyeballs. There was nothing there, nothing but the darkness of the empty street and the squalling wind. A hand touched his arm. He jerked round, spilling some of the red wine onto his chest where it dribbled like thin blood among the hairs. Hilary, also naked, stepped in front of him and circled his waist with her arms, pressing herself against him.

'Mind if I have some of your wine?' she said.

With long, slow strokes, she used her tongue to lick the red liquid stains from his chest. She made a thorough job of it, moving her head back to check if she had missed any and then moving in again. The pain behind Fyfe's nose was soothed away. He let the curtains fall closed and leaned back against the wall to support himself while he enjoyed the sensation.

'I thought I saw someone out there in the street,' he said.

96

She lifted her head to look up at him and raised her eyebrows questioningly. 'Who do you think it might be?'

'Your jealous husband?'

She shook her head, the tip of her tongue tracing over the curve of the hollow of his throat. 'I doubt it.'

'Oh?'

'More likely to be my jealous lover.' She began to pull him down to the floor. 'My other lover. He should be jealous too, very jealous.'

Fyfe was suddenly very cold. He realized just how little he knew about Hilary. Nothing about her history, her background, her upbringing, her politics, her passions, her prejudices, her secrets, her mental state. Despite their present intimacy they had had little but superficial social contact, not more than a few hours in each other's company. There had been an initial meeting at a party, mutual attraction, a couple of half-hearted kisses, a long gap, then a brief swimming session. And so to bed. Crossing the line.

Fyfe lay on his back on the carpet with Hilary astride him, her hands on her hips. The battery charger was at his head, its red light glowing, a warning that he would soon have to prepare himself to return to another world, far removed from this one of complete and total self-absorption.

Above him, Hilary ran a hand over her forehead to drag her hair back. Her nostrils flared and her eyes glittered. A darting pain behind Fyfe's nose climbed towards a rapid crescendo. He moaned involuntarily as she pressed down on him with her full weight, the pain inside his head cancelled out by the pleasure infusing the rest of his body.

'You like that, don't you?' Hilary whispered, not expecting an answer.

28

Wednesday: 22.56

The flickering pictures on the silent television screen created moving shadows on the faces of the three men watching them.

Connor Harper pressed the fast-forward button and the pictures accelerated into an impossibly fast comical storm of flying arms and legs. Harper killed the speed and the picture instantly re-solved itself into a tangle of bare bodies all climbing and clawing over each other.

'No wonder little Sarah ran away from us,' Harper said. 'It looks like she didn't hate Bruce Davidson enough to refuse to star in his films.'

Harper, Crichton and Munro were in an equipment-cluttered side office known as the clarty room because of its function. They were copying the videos taken from Davidson's deserted flat onto police-issue tapes to be held as evidence. They had seen six different women involved at various stages in different home-made blue movies, and at least three men. One of the women was Sarah, clearly recognizable although she had shrunk and withered a lot since her starring days, and another two were the poison victims Virginia and Belinda, Ginny and Bel, tattoos and all. They thought that one of the men was David-son himself but couldn't be sure. Lots of freeze frames and close-screen comparisons with the poor quality polaroid photograph faxed up from London didn't confirm his identity. As far as they could make out there was no sign, from comparisons with their photographs, of either Scott Anderson or the bus driver Billy Stoddart. But it was close to midnight and they had been through less than half the videos. Crichton and Munro settled down in their chairs with their feet up to copy and watch the remainder.

'It's a dirty job but somebody's got to do it,' Crichton said, handing one can of beer to Munro and cracking open another for himself. 'And besides, you're never too old to learn.'

'See you in the canteen for breakfast,' Munro said, tilting his head back and drinking.

There was also another poison victim to add to the list. A train cleaner at King's Cross who went mad in public and dropped down dead in a dramatic fashion in the middle of the station. The routine reference to the National Poisons Register linked her to the case. Then it became clear that she was the woman who had tried to revive Davidson when he was found unconscious on board a train the previous day. The Met speculated that her attempt to give him the kiss of life which, doctors said, had probably saved him, had also been responsible for communicating the poison into her bloodstream. Now Katherine something or other was dead and Davidson was running loose. How many more was he going to take with him?

Harper left Crichton and Munro to it and got a taxi home, resisting the strong temptation to try a late-night visit to Kelly in the hope that she might take pity on him. He knew the time was not yet right for him to be accepted back. He had not done sufficient penance after the disastrous holiday. He didn't even consider throwing himself on the mercy of his estranged wife Anne. He had no chance there. He was on his own.

The sight of all the willing, writhing bodies on the videos had unsettled Harper. He felt sorry for little Sarah who had been transformed from a busty, healthily rounded female as seen on the videos into a pathetic husk of a child-woman. It was drugs probably that had caused it, or disease. But what depressed him most was not the individual case, but the fact that Sarah's existence was just an accelerated form of everyone's life, no matter how righteous or how dissolute. She may have deliberately pressed the fast-forward self-destruct button on herself but she was acting out what was a universal condition.

Then there were the two dead girls captured on video so soon before fate caught up with them. On video, they were still healthy, still well rounded, and their dead bodies suggested that they had yet to follow Sarah down the road of no return. They might have been saved, but where were they now? They were victims of the universal condition, lying in sub-zero compartments at the mortuary, their bodies artificially prevented from decaying until he could work out what had happened to them and to the mad dog, the weekend sailor with his weeping widow, and the bus driver along the street, and then the would-be Samaritan in London. Where was the sense in it all? It was possible that the video passage that linked them all was running through the recorder now as he got out of his car and pulled the collar of his coat up around his ears. Thin, jagged strips of black cloud were moving across a grey sky. The city seemed deserted, bereft of human life, as if he, scurrying across the road, was the only survivor of a sudden holocaust and everybody else was neatly stored in body-sized drawers one on top of the other in the mortuary.

Harper didn't switch the lights on in his empty home. The darkness seemed appropriate to the fog of depression that enveloped him. He had survived the day without a drink because he had concentrated hard on the investigation. It had not been too difficult because his mind had been fully occupied and he had not had any time to think. But now it was late and the weariness of his limbs was in direct contrast to the alertness of his mind, which was wandering alarmingly in all sorts of weird and less than wonderful directions. He tried to concentrate on the murder investigation but he kept having visions of Kelly's floppy bunny slippers and seeing the cute rabbit faces bare their teeth to snarl at him.

In the dark, Harper followed a familiar route across the carpet, avoiding the furniture, straight to where he kept the alcohol in the press at the side of the cold fireplace. There was whisky, vodka, gin, brandy and rum. He chose a bottle of port because he hated the taste, and slumped down in the armchair, still wearing his coat. He didn't hesitate. He drank from the bottle, grimacing as the sweetness hit the back of his throat but forcing himself to swallow. Initial distaste turned to a pleasing sense of inner warmth as the sweetness faded. He took another swig, churned it like a mouthwash, and swallowed. Before he knew it the bottle was empty. It didn't matter, there was plenty more. He hunted through the cupboard for the rum. This time he went to the kitchen and filled a pint glass, half and half, with rum and milk. The physical pleasure now had changed to a need. He needed to drink so that he wouldn't have to think. And it was working fast. Back in the living room, he slumped in the chair, willing himself to merge into the darkness that surrounded him. He pulled the collar of his coat up, shrinking into its heaviness to prevent himself shivering, imagining it was Kelly draped all around him, feeling the exhaustion that made his body lie so still finally reach his brain and cause it to slow down. He took another sip of the rum and milk, spilling some down his chin. He wiped it clean and licked the back of his hand. It didn't matter. There was plenty more.

29

Fyfe crept away from Hilary's house. He was wearing his dark glasses and almost tiptoeing so as not to be noticed by the neighbours. The morning was just turning, insipid daylight leaking down from a pale sky. There was a smir of rain in the air and an irregular wind that seemed to be swirling only at ankle level. Another man walked along the pavement towards Fyfe. He was dressed similarly, was wearing tinted glasses, hadn't shaved, and was carrying the same kind of holdall bag in his right hand. In a fleeting moment of male companionship their eyes met and the two men nodded to each other, smiled in mutual understanding and passed by without stopping or exchanging a word.

Before he had left Hilary's house, he had taken a few minutes in the bathroom to splash cold water on his face and some aftershave on his stubbly cheeks. The bruising round his eyes had receded a lot to become hardly noticeable, just a yellow puffiness and a couple of purple streaks. His nose was tender and felt much more swollen than it looked. The cut on it was dark red. He collected his recharged mobile phone and, with a quick glance through the curtains to check there was no one around outside, went down the stairs and out into the street.

For Fyfe, it had been a long and sleepless night. Hilary had been a demanding partner and when she had slept she had tossed and turned and kicked restlessly, effectively preventing him from doing the same. Wrapped up in a single sheet they had talked for hours too, though he couldn't remember much of what had actually been said. It was inconsequential chatter, small talk about favourite colours and favourite foods and favourite phobias and favourite places they had visited. Finally, to avoid a more grown-up conversation during an enforced sit-down breakfast in the harsh light of day, he had made his excuses and slipped away, leaving Hilary sprawled face down diagonally across the big bed, the whole scene reflected in the three sections of mirror glass that made up the doors of the fitted wardrobe. What was it Hilary had said to him about having to be careful because her other lover was spying on her? She had been joking. Or had she? Had the other lover stood in this same doorway, still warm from her touch and damp from her sweat, admiring her lying on the bed? Had he been running away too, a spirit of the night unwilling to face Hilary when the dawn broke and a different set of rules of engagement applied?

Outside, Fyfe walked for more than half a mile, constantly looking back over his shoulder but never seeing another person, before he came to a main road with moving traffic. While he waited for a taxi to appear he phoned the incident room's direct line at police headquarters and got no answer. He rang the main switchboard and they tried to put him through but there was still no answer. He insisted they keep trying and eventually, just as Fyfe was about to give up in disgust, Pete Crichton's sleepily irritated voice came on the line.

'Morning, Pete,' Fyfe said with false heartiness. 'I'm back.'

'Where have you been?'

'Having my nose remodelled. Where the fuck do you think I've been?'

Crichton became more alert. There was a scraping noise as he sat up, the sound of paper flapping. 'Sorry, sir,' he said. 'We've been up all night.'

'So have I.'

'We were going through evidence in the inquiry.'

Fyfe had no intention of explaining why he had not slept so he ignored the natural pause in the conversation. Crichton continued: 'One of the tapes unravelled inside the guts of the recorder and jammed it so we're having to wait for a technician to come and fix it.'

'What tapes?' Fyfe asked, feeling the side of his bag to check that he had the video cassettes that Davidson had been carrying on his trip to London. He had totally forgotten about them till that moment.

'We found a bunch of blue movies in Davidson's flat and the principal stars included our two female victims. We know it was them. They are easily identified by the tattoos on their bums.'

'Excellent detective work. Now we're getting somewhere. Has Connor shown his face yet?'

'No, sir. He went home late last night.' Fyfe recognized the reluctant hesitation in Crichton's speech and knew what it meant: that he was covering up for a colleague. 'He was pretty knackered. Been putting in a lot of hours.'

'Don't we all,' Fyfe said, remembering that Harper had only just returned from holiday. 'Hurry up that video technician. I'll be there as soon as I can.'

Fyfe unzipped the bag to convince himself Davidson's video cassettes were still in it. They were, wrapped in a plastic Safeways bag. He should have guessed they were important before now. If Davidson had gone to the trouble of taking these two tapes with him on his escape to London, he reasoned, they must have something particularly interesting on them. He stood impatiently at the side of the road, watching the traffic become more frequent but not once providing the sight of an elusive taxi. He began to wonder about Connor Harper and Crichton's knee-jerk defensive allusion to him being knackered. That was a coded way of referring to Harper's potential drink problem. Most of his fellow detectives were aware of his vulnerability in this area but none would ever mention it out loud. They all drank themselves, bar a small unrepresentative minority, and there was too much of the 'There but for the grace of God go I' in everybody's attitude to land Harper in trouble by lodging a formal complaint. They would cover for him at every opportunity until it became too much to hide. Then, but only then, would he be thrown to the wolves.

Fyfe empathized strongly. He had gone through the same experience himself. Been there, done it. As a DI, with his marriage breaking up and his girlfriend close to a nervous breakdown, he had dived right to the bottom of the bottle and been found drunk and incapable in the squad room one night. It was all so long ago. His career had only been rescued by the forgiving nature of a Chief Constable who magnanimously refused to condemn him outright and sack him. Instead, he had given him the second chance he required to pull himself together and survive, even gaining promotion to chief inspector against the odds. Sir Duncan Morrison was still the Chief Constable, still displaying the same sense of moral superiority that had allowed him to be Fyfe's personal saviour. He still believed Fyfe was the model policeman; once flawed but now restored. If only he knew the truth, that Fyfe had learned to survive by breaking the law at least as often as he upheld it. He had kept the illicit proceeds of an armed robbery, even now a couple of hundred thousand pounds in used and untraceable banknotes was hidden beneath the boards of his garden shed in old biscuit tins. And lately he had organized and eagerly participated in a violent attack on his erring son-in-law because there was no sanction available to the law to make him pay adequate recompense for what he had done to Fyfe's daughter. Such behaviour was in part a kind of revenge, he told himself, for being so helplessly indebted to Sir Duncan. He had taken to carrying round his letter of resignation, waiting for the opportunity to hand it over and release himself from the obligation. He felt in his jacket pockets, searching for the letter. He could not find it, could not think what he had done with it. He hadn't handed it in. The right moment had never come. Not yet anyway.

He glanced over his shoulder. The hairs on his neck were bristling with the suspicion that he was being followed. More and more people were appearing, spilling out of doorways and coming round corners. He thought back to the previous night and the flickering movement he had seen, the head jerking out of sight behind the parked car. Had it really been Hilary's other lover? Maybe he was already recruiting an obliging stranger in a pub to come after Fyfe and do him some damage. Collateral damage, the military called it, when innocent civilians were caught in a crossfire. Except Fyfe wasn't a civilian in this case. He was in the front line, one of the poor bloody infantry.

He looked up at the street name on the building above him. Harper's home address was not far away. He calculated that he could walk there easily in about fifteen minutes. He might as well walk there and get Harper to give him a lift. If a taxi came he would grab it and head straight to the office and get on with his work. If not, he would go to Harper's home and see if it was possible to save him from self-destruction. If Harper was there Fyfe would wake him, admonish him gently, ensure that he got in to work on time, offer him some paternal advice and the kind of professional protection Fyfe would have been so glad of when it was he who was having the problem.

He saw a taxi approach and stepped to the edge of the pavement, raising an arm to hail it, but the light was out and there was the silhouette of somebody in the back. Fyfe cursed and stepped back. The taxi went on past, its icily damp slipstream making him turn his face to the side. He looked in both directions along the street. The traffic was flowing in a constant stream now. An old woman went by walking a tiny dog that was done up in a red and blue knitted coat. She smiled at him and he automatically smiled back. Otherwise, nobody in the street was paying the slightest bit of attention to him. Fyfe put his head down and started to walk.

30

Thursday: 07.34

At the back of the converted farm steading the battered oil drum stood in the centre of a circle of scorched earth, red flames glowing through the holes punched in its sides. A fat column of smoke rose diagonally and drifted away at head height, pushed to one side by the wind. The heads of a gaggle of guardian geese watched silently from the safety of the surrounding dew-wet long grass. Further out, a parliament of crows wheeled above the branches of the big shoulder-to-shoulder trees that screened the constantly busy bypass.

Michael Guthrie had always kept the administrative records of his business meticulously. Now he was equally meticulous in destroying them. He wore his customary work apron as he walked back and forth from the door to the drum. His boots rubbed against the backs of his ankles, aggravating the skin. He moved slowly because his joints were stiff and sore with advancing age. He ensured that the bundles of papers were broken up as he poured them into the fire so that every individual page would be consumed. He had begun the task in the darkness before dawn and continued it as the pale light of daybreak changed the colours of the countryside around him, allowing the natural greens and browns and yellows to emerge. Every few minutes the wind found its way in through the holes in the drum to fan the greedy flames, causing an upward shower of black, burned paper flakes. The shelves and filing cabinets and occasional cardboard boxes in the room Guthrie used as an office were gradually emptied in the space of three hours until ashes were almost spilling over the rim of the drum and there was nothing left to burn.

Guthrie brushed back his grey hair and stared up at the circling crows. He remembered watching his father doing exactly what he was doing one Sunday long ago in another place. He had been a ten-year-old child, hiding in long grass like the geese, aware that his father's strange behaviour was connected to the baby he had been promised, a little sister who had been born behind closed doors, but whom, they now told him, he would never see. He had not been allowed to go to Florence's funeral. Instead he was taken care of for the day by his Uncle James who gave him ice cream and anything he wanted. It was a sunny day and they went boating in a public park. The young boy looked down into the water where his reflection was clouded by shoals of tiny tadpoles. When he cupped his hands and scooped some up the plump black creatures wriggled on his skin as the water dribbled away between his fingers.

Guthrie knew the burning had been on a Sunday because he remembered that his father had been wearing his best church-going clothes, the white shirt with the separate collar, only ever worn on that day. His father was a church elder. He walked down the aisle each week to gather the plates when the collection was taken. He handed out hymn books at the door and took them back at the end of the service. He sometimes went over to the manse to help the minister write his sermons. Every evening at home, the boy was encouraged to say his prayers and to thank God for all the small mercies that made life so good, and every Sunday night his father would read from the huge family Bible that had been handed down to him from his own grandfather. The Bible was burned that day, its pages ripped out in handfuls and tossed contemptuously into the fire. His father's pristine white shirt became stained by the smoke. When he wiped his face with his hand he left black marks. And all the time his mother was at the window of the house, watching too, her eyes red and troubled with the grief and shock of the stillbirth which, the boy thought later, was supposed to be purged in the flames. There had been more than paper in his father's bonfire, the house furniture had been tossed onto it too, and the boxes from the attic containing a myriad of mysterious things he would never know about. That evening in the silent house his father sat at the fireside and stared into space. When the time came for the customary Bible reading he did not move. 'Don't believe it, Michael,' he said when the boy shook his arm to remind him. 'Don't believe any of it.'

They left the next day, the family's belongings in two suitcases and the leather schoolbag he carried on his back. That had been the start of the break-up of the family. It was a clear dividing line. After the fire, once they had moved to a new place, his father and mother never stopped shouting at each other, fighting with each other, something that had never happened before. Neither of them had touched alcohol before but they began drinking heavily. It was all to forget the stillborn sister who had destroyed the happy family they had once been. They stopped going to church, stopped searching for a reason. Bible stories were replaced by tirades of bad language, and random violent attacks. Self-pity loaded the blame for their situation onto Florence. It was bad, hopeless. As soon as he was old enough, the young boy left home and tried to forget them. He began reading the Bible, searching for the message his father had missed, the bit that would make sense of it all. When his parents died he did not go to their funerals. Instead he burned his birth certificate and everything else he could find that connected him to them. And still he read the Bible until he had memorized almost every passage, waiting patiently but never managing to find an explanation for what had gone wrong.

Guthrie had been staring at the burning paper in the oil drum. The heat from the glowing pile of ashes was intense on his face and eyeballs. He stepped back and stood with his hands in the single pocket of his apron, remembering how the first girl had looked exactly the way he had always imagined

Florence would look, her nakedness enhancing his conception of her innocence. That was the devilish trick that had trapped him. He should have known better, should have realized what was happening. Dead people didn't grow old. They became idealized visions. It was almost half a century since Florence had been born, but born dead. She had never lived. She had never existed. He should have known better. He should never have believed there was an answer to be found. Too late now. Far too late now.

31

Thursday: 08.10

It was a modern five-storey block built on a corner site where five roads joined in an untidy crossroads controlled by a confusing array of traffic lights. Fyfe knew that Harper stayed on the ground floor in the right-hand flat. He could see his door through the reinforced glass of the exterior safety door. He had been here before, dumping a paralytic Harper the night after his wife and kids walked out on him. And then another night when Harper had insisted on inviting him in and introducing his new girlfriend, an incredibly young-looking lassie with dyed blonde hair, immaculate long fingernails and expensively engineered teeth. Fyfe had fallen for her instantly but had never seen her again. What was her name again? Kitty? Kathy? Caroline? Catriona?

Fyfe checked the windows facing the street and saw that all the curtains were open. There was no answer at first when he pressed the button under Harper's name on the intercom panel at the exterior door. From outside, the buzzing was a distant sound but it would be much louder, much more insistent, and more demanding inside. On a hunch, he kept his finger pressed firmly for more than five minutes, long beyond the time any visitor with average patience would have reasonably lasted. If there was someone there and he was still breathing he would have to answer eventually. A postman with an unwieldy bag on his hip used a key to enter, not once looking directly at Fyfe but ensuring that the door was locked behind him, running up the stairs three at a time to begin his deliveries at the top of the block and work down.

Fyfe sighed as he removed his numb finger from the stainless-steel button and sucked the tip to warm it up. He was about to turn away when an incomprehensible crackle came from the loudspeaker and the exterior door clicked to indicate that he had access. Fyfe entered and got to Harper's door just as it opened. Harper stood there blinking and frowning, not seeming to know who Fyfe was at all until he had peered at him very closely through pinprick eyes screwed up among bunches of fine wrinkles to keep out the bulk of the pain-inducing light. He was wearing his coat as if he had just arrived at the outside rather than the inside of the door. Fyfe smelled urine and saw a tell-tale stain on the inside leg of Harper's trousers. The blast of fetid sweetness from his breath made Fyfe cover his nose.

'It's you,' Harper said finally, staring at the cut on Fyfe's nose. 'What happened to you?'

'It's me. Take me as you find me.'

'I thought it might be Kelly.'

Kelly, that was her name, Fyfe remembered. An appropriate name that for some reason she seemed to suit very well. The way Harper pronounced it was infused with disappointment. What had a nice young girl like her ever seen in a wreck of a human being like Connor Harper? The same question could be asked of him and Hilary, he supposed, except that he had long since packed in emotionally charged love affairs in favour of the infinitely less complicated lustful versions.

'You should be grateful it's me, Connor,' Fyfe said. 'If the lovely Kelly saw you in a state like this your arse really would be out her window.'

'Just had a drink,' Harper said, slurring the words badly. 'I was on my own so I had to have a little drink.'

'I know the feeling.'

'No harm in it, is there? Would you like a drink, sir. There's some left.'

109

'No thanks.'

Holding onto the door and the wall, Harper shrugged and swayed. He let go of the door and put his hand to his head. His eyes rolled up to display the sickly yellow whites and for a moment it looked as if he was going to pass out. But he recovered quickly and started to go through the whole process of blinking and frowning again as though he was seeing Fyfe for the first time. The postman appeared at Fyfe's shoulder, again ignoring him as if he wasn't there, and without a word handed two envelopes to Harper who reached out and took them automatically. The postman walked away, still shuffling through his next batch of letters. Fyfe put his hand on Harper's chest and pushed him backwards into the flat.

'I think you've had enough to drink for the time being, don't you, Connor?'

'Probably,' he admitted, nodding stupidly.

'Do you think you're up to going to work?'

'Probably.'

'Think positively.'

'Definitely.'

'Come on then. Let's get you ready.'

Harper sat on a chair at the table in the kitchen, stretched out his arms on the surface and put his head down. Fyfe switched on the kettle and found a jar of instant coffee. There was little else in the cupboards beyond a few tins of peaches and half a stale loaf of bread. The fridge had some instant meals in its freezer compartment and cans of Seven Up on the shelves. The lack of food made Fyfe hungry. He wished he had stayed at Hilary's. She had offered to make him a cooked breakfast. She would have waited on him, fussed over him, seen that he had got a good nutritional start to the day. But he had needed to get away to be alone. Next time, he promised himself, it would be different. A full breakfast would be an essential item on the menu.

Fyfe went through to the bathroom and turned on the taps to fill the bath. There was no hot water. He cleared the collection of sponges and shampoo bottles from the edge and piled them in the sink. He went back to the kitchen. Steam was pouring upwards from the boiling kettle and Harper was still slumped over the table. Fyfe pulled him upright by the neck of his coat, taking the chance to slip off one arm as he rose to a vertical position.

'Nice hot bath, Connor,' he coaxed, wrestling with the other arm. 'That'll sort you out.'

Harper, either half awake or half unconscious, mumbled something unintelligible. He allowed Fyfe to continue to undress him. The pair made awkward progress between kitchen and bathroom and by the time they got there Harper was down to his vest, boxer shorts and socks. The bath was more than half full when Fyfe turned off the taps. He stood back as Harper stepped into the water. He had both feet in before he realized just how cold it was. He stopped in the middle of the act of sitting down, all his weight on his arms on either side of the bath. His eyes opened wide and he looked questioningly at Fyfe who smiled encouragingly and chopped sharply at the vulnerable elbow nearest to him. It gave way and Harper splashed down into the bath, slopping a huge wave over the side. Fyfe avoided the overflow as best he could, put his hand on Harper's forehead and dunked him under the water totally. Fyfe danced backwards as Harper came up like a breaching whale, spluttering and gasping. His skin tone had changed from pale white to rosy pink. He thrashed around frantically, spraying water in all directions, but could find no purchase on the smooth surface of the bath. He slid under again and came up gasping even more desperately.

Fyfe closed the bathroom door and listened to the noises from within. He was a little wet around the waist and the shins but not too bad. His feeling of depression had lifted because he believed he had acted wisely and honourably. A sudden rush of optimism cleared his fuzzy thoughts. He had saved Connor Harper from himself, just as he had been saved when he was almost too far gone to care. The shock treatment would bring Harper to his senses. All that time ago Sir Duncan had taken Fyfe by the scruff of the neck, marched him down to the basement and thrown him under a cold shower, holding the door shut so that he couldn't get out. It had worked for him. Now history was repeating itself after a fashion. Fyfe grinned at the memory. He was a saviour. Now there would be someone obligated to him for the rest of his life. That felt good, uncomfortably good. Once Harper was fully recovered, how he would hate him.

111

32

Thursday: 09.01

Gordon Collins was the new boy in the van; Bobby Thomas, yet to celebrate his nineteenth birthday, the experienced old-timer with ten months on the job behind him.

'We call this bloke the Keeper,' Thomas explained. 'As in zoo keeper. Get it? Pythons, snakes, lizards, tarantulas, geckos, toads, frogs. You name it, the Keeper's definitely got it in one of his glass tanks. The guy is a serious loonie. Used to run a big pet shop, then he moved to live out here all alone and breed them. He talks to them, you know. I've seen him. Loopy as my granny's perm. Stay close, young Gordie. Don't get separated or he'll have you set up in one of those tanks to use in a breeding experiment.'

Collins casually pulled at his row of six earrings to hide his nervousness. Ever since his brother had slipped a fat spider into a glass of lemonade when he was a child he had had an embarrassing fear of creepy-crawlies and things that slithered on their bellies. Every time he saw one it brought back the sensation of the squirming thing in his mouth and the sticky sweet liquid oozing out as he bit down before he realized what was happening. When he had applied for the job at the pet store he had assumed he would be working with cute cats and dogs; rats and mice were more or less okay by him as well. He liked furry things and, by and large, they liked him back. It was cold-blooded, scaly reptiles and many-legged insects he had a phobia about but by the time he realized they were part of the package it was too late for him to back down. What could he say? No thanks. I'll not bother with the job, I'm a wee bit scared of spiders you see. No, he couldn't let on or they would laugh at him. Besides he needed the job and the cash, such as it was, so he gritted his teeth and grinned bravely. For his first week he had concentrated on the rabbits and the hamsters, trying to establish himself as a bit of a specialist so that he would not have to go near the horrible scuttling stuff. But it wasn't possible to avoid it altogether, and he managed to survive a shift cleaning out the lizards' cages. This was the first time he had been sent out in the van. They told him it was a promotion.

'Guy I took over from as driver used to say the Keeper was a bit of a Dr Frankenstein,' Collins said, nodding to confirm his own statement. 'Said the Keeper once tried to persuade him to bring out girls so that he could experiment on them. Genetic experiments. You know the kind of thing. Breed them with monkeys and dogs and see what comes out. It's true.'

'Did you believe him?' Collins asked, still trying to work out how seriously to take what Thomas told him.

'Naw. The Keeper's harmless and big Brucie always was a bullshitter.'

'What happened to him?'

'Brucie? He was last seen being digested by a nineteen-foot Burmese python.'

Thomas cackled and had to wipe stray saliva from the corner of his mouth. Collins decided not to take anything he said seriously. 'Only kidding. Brucie was all right. He taught me the ropes. Got himself sacked for flogging freelance chipmunks on the side. Could have made more with parrots. Folk pay fortunes for parrots.'

The Keeper's house was just off the city bypass, reached by a muddy track and screened by an earth bank and a stand of old colourful trees just beginning their annual leaf-shedding process. The sound of the invisible traffic was a background oceanic murmur. The house was actually a converted farm steading made up of a collection of low-eaved buildings and a jumble of doors and windows all joined together in the original horseshoe shape. A flock of half a dozen plump grey and white geese emerged from the long grass as the van approached and effectively halted its progress. The geese honked triumphantly and marched back into the grass.

'Do they bite?' Collins asked.

'Oh yes. Put your leg out there and they'll have it off. The Keeper's not much bothered by trespassers.'

'Do geese have teeth?'

113

Thomas thought about it. 'Don't know.'

'Where are they going now?'

'They recognize the van so they're letting us pass. Pretty smart for things with such small brains, huh?'

Thomas rolled the van forward the last few yards to the main door and switched off the engine when it was parked directly behind a smaller and much more battered pick-up van.

'Come on then. He'll have the stuff ready. He's always well organized, I'll say that for him. Let's go and get it.'

Collins followed his partner, jumping down to step carefully through the mud and around the van. The smell of burning was in the air, a column of smoke just visible over the roof. Thomas didn't knock, just shoved the door open with his shoulder and went straight in, shouting loudly for Mr Guthrie. Collins assumed that was the Keeper's real name. The ceilings were low, the corridors long. They turned right, then left and right again, passed through an open glass-roofed courtyard full of thin trees and undergrowth populated by screeching birds, and eventually came out into a slightly smaller and much quieter area with another glass roof and a warmly humid atmosphere that reminded him of early morning on the beach at Tenerife. On every side, Collins suddenly realized, he was surrounded by walls of glass tanks stacked one on top of each other. Some seemed empty. In others, things moved and watched him. The nearest tank had a row of four smooth-skinned frogs perched on a stone, wide mouths spread in human-style comical smiles. On the roof the wind made dry leaves scratch and drift. In another tank there was a rustling sound and a snake raised its head. Collins felt his shirt stick to the small of his back where sweat was gathering.

'Keep the door shut tight,' a voice commanded.

'Sure thing, Mr Guthrie,' Thomas replied. 'It's me. I know the score.'

The Keeper was on their left, standing on a wheeled kick-ladder and reaching into a third-tier tank like a librarian retrieving a book, except that he was dangling half a dead mouse by its hind leg. He dropped the mouse and lifted a yellow snake out, pinching it between finger and thumb behind its tiny head, and stared at it sadly. He was a skinny, round-shouldered grey-haired man with bushy eyebrows and a thick paintbrush moustache that hid his mouth totally. He wore a knee-length butcher's apron over a green tartan shirt and faded denim jeans tucked inside laceless boots. His watery eyes had dark bags underneath as though the liquid was leaking out and collecting in reservoirs there. He looked very old, very tired, and very sad. Collins felt sorry for him.

'This is Gordon Collins, Mr Guthrie,' Thomas said. 'He's learning the system with me today.'

The Keeper replaced the snake in the tank and came down the ladder backwards, growing even smaller in stature. He turned and examined Collins with his sad eyes while tapping the tip of his nose with a knuckle. He nodded as if acknowledging that he understood, but Collins couldn't work out what he thought there might be to understand. Something else moved in another tank, a flash of green and brown that was instantly gone, and he couldn't stop himself flinching.

'You take over from Bruce and this boy takes over from you, is that it?'

'Reckon it is, Mr Guthrie.'

'Ever hear from Bruce?'

'Never did.'

'No.' The Keeper sighed and uttered what sounded like a laugh. 'Never did. Probably never will. Have you read the Bible, Gordon?'

The question was so unexpected that Collins grunted as if he had been punched in the stomach when he tried to answer. His parents had forced him to go to Sunday School but not for too long. He never went to church. He couldn't think what to say. He just stared at the deeply scored lines on the old man's face and wondered if his lips moved behind the moustache when he spoke. There was no sign of it. The voice just emerged.

'To everything there is a season, and a time to every purpose under the heaven,' the Keeper said wearily. 'A time to be born and a time to die.'

'Yes, sir,' Collins said, trying to ignore Thomas who was capering about behind the Keeper's back, tapping his index finger against his forehead and sticking out his tongue.

'That's what I do. I make the time here for all these creatures to be born.' He waved his hand around the encircling tanks and let it come to rest on Collins's shoulder. 'I oversee the births and send them out from here. That is my role. Later they die, but that is not my fault. I can hardly be held responsible for the great and endless cycle of nature, can I?'

'No, sir.'

The Keeper looked up at the roof, tilting his head so far back Collins was able to see the contours of his lips under the flap of the moustache. Something somewhere in one of the tanks plopped into water. The row of smiling frogs sat motionless. Gradually the Keeper moved his head back until he was looking at Collins again.

'Birth is what I do,' he said. 'Birth, the positive side of life on earth. Not death. That is nothing to do with me.'

'Good.'

'I have plenty of life for you today; young macaws, zebra finches, parrots, a host of garter snake hatchlings, other assorted snakes, a particularly beautiful orange-toed lizard that I am proud of. If it wasn't for me, none of these creatures would be alive.' The twisting of his facial muscles suggested that he was smiling. 'I have life for you. Life in many varied and marvellous forms. Lots of life. As ordered. Ready for delivery.'

The Keeper led them back through the noisy birds in the aviary. He stopped for a few moments to check on a sick-looking cockatiel that was sitting hunched and miserable on its perch and they had to wait. Then he took them back along the corridors to the main door. Alongside it was another less obvious door that gave access to a storeroom packed with pierced livestock boxes and bird cages all ready to be carried to the van. When Collins lifted the boxes to take them outside he could feel the living things inside moving around. While they worked the Keeper stood by the doorway, watching them carefully, tapping each box as it was shifted and ticking it off a checklist. With each stroke of the pen he repeated another biblical epigram.

'A time to weep and a time to laugh.'

Tick.

'A time to mourn and a time to dance.'

Tick.

'A time to get and a time to lose.'

Tick.

'A time to love and a time to hate.'

Tick.

'A time to be born and a time to die.'

Tick.

When the back of the van was full the Keeper handed over the documentation and stuffed his copies into the pocket of the apron. He retreated inside to join his birds and his snakes and his lizards and his smiling frogs. Bobby Thomas started up the engine and reversed out. The guardian geese honked in the grass, long necks sticking up like marker flags.

'Well?' Thomas asked. 'What did you make of that?'

'He is a bit strange, isn't he?' Collins replied.

'Seriously strange,' Thomas said. 'Didn't I tell you? He's aged a lot since I last saw him. I think he's getting crazier with every passing day. If that's possible.'

'Is he a religious fanatic then?'

'An independent fanatic. Once told me he would burn down every church in the country if he had the chance.'

'Harmless though?'

'Maybe.'

33

Thursday: 09.43

Connor Harper surfaced from his enforced immersion in the freezing cold water of the bath and sorted himself out. He was embarrassed at what had happened to him. He must have been in a really bad state to piss himself while sleeping in the arm-chair, but in a way he was pleased that he now had nothing left to hide. Fyfe knew everything. There were many stories about Fyfe, always whispered behind his back, that he had been a really bad heavy drinker, a liability who assaulted suspects and ruined difficult investigations by sloppy and inaccurate work. The story went that after a particularly unsavoury episode he had been given one last chance to redeem himself. He had seized it gratefully and changed totally to become a model detective, looked up to and respected by all his colleagues. He still drank, still was by all accounts a lecherous womanizer, but the trick Fyfe seemed to have learned was to keep all these things separate and in proportion, not to let them combine and take him over. He stayed in control. Now, Harper realized, he too had been given one last chance to turn himself around. There were no second last chances. He decided he was ready to make the effort to seize it gratefully.

Harper found a change of underwear and put on the only other suit he possessed, a charcoal-grey affair that he kept aside for funerals. Fyfe was waiting for him in the kitchen with strong coffee and plenty of advice on the subjects of drink and women, mostly on why neither was worth it the morning after. The catch was that it was unreasonable to expect such a simple truth to be appreciated the night before when such considerations were the last thing on anyone's mind. Harper told him about Sarah Smith disappearing into the night, about the blue movies she starred in, and about his girlfriend Kelly flinging the bunch of flowers in his face. Just speaking about made it seem very matter of fact and ordinary.

They got a taxi to a street where shopkeepers were stocking the fruit and vegetable stalls on the pavement outside their premises, adjusting the individual items and standing back to judge the effect like artists setting up still-life portraits. Fyfe led Harper down into a basement barber's shop where a huge Italian called Sergio waved an open razor and sang along to tapes of Puccini operas. Fyfe was obviously a regular customer but Harper couldn't understand a word the big man said to him. He had already shaved but Sergio sat him in a dentist-style chair, tilted him backwards at a steep angle and shaved him closer still. Then he wrapped his head in hot towels while Fyfe was seen to. They re-emerged into the street with tingling cheeks and absolutely no excuse not to have perfectly clear heads.

He had hardly eaten anything in the days since getting back from his holiday in Greece. So Harper took it as a good sign that he was hungry. At the police canteen he and Fyfe ordered fried breakfasts, doused them with brown sauce, and ate them facing each other over a formica-topped table while white-shirted uniforms going on and off shift swirled around them. Between mouthfuls Fyfe told him how he had been a heavy drinker who had identified and solved his own problem. It was all a matter of judgement and self-control, Fyfe said. Harper agreed, resolving to remain in control of his own destiny. No more rum and milk sessions because the gorgeous young Kelly was in a huff with him. Fyfe approved.

They climbed the stairs to the incident room. Harper sat down at his desk and began to shuffle papers aimlessly as the ever-present and reliable Matthewson handed Fyfe a typewritten brief to bring him up to date on the case. Crichton and Munro were asleep somewhere after being up all night and the technician had not appeared to fix the video equipment in the clarty room. Fyfe remembered Davidson's videos and the photographs he had brought up with him from London and realized he had left the bag at Harper's house. He swore under his breath and didn't tell anyone. He read the prepared brief, noting the divergence between the tattooed girls and Bruce Davidson, who were obviously linked, and fellow poison victims Scott Anderson and his neighbour Billy Stoddart, the kamikaze bus driver. There had to be some connection as with the unfortunate train cleaner in London who had done her citizen's duty and given Davidson the kiss of life only to end up dead. What had Scott and Billy done to deserve their fate?

'Any dogs in the films?' Fyfe asked.

'Hundreds of them,' Matthewson said. 'Some really good-looking girls as well.'

'No, I meant real dogs as in canine dogs.'

'I don't think we've seen anything like that yet.'

'The late Rex doesn't feature then?'

'Not yet but we've got a few tapes to go.'

The phone rang. Fyfe answered and found a Professor McDougall asking for Harper and introducing himself in tones of hushed excitement. Fyfe switched the call and listened in as he ran his finger down the page to find the name and discover what his relevance was. There it was; professor of toxicology. Just the man they needed.

'I have identified the poison,' McDougall told Harper. 'You should come round and I will explain the details. You will be amazed, Mr Fyfe, I promise you. Fascinating, it is. Quite fascinating. Trust me, you'll hardly believe your ears.'

34

Thursday: 10.12

Kate threw up noisily into the sink, leaning over from where she sat on the toilet with her dressing gown round her shoulders and her knickers at her ankles. She hadn't been able to eat anything the previous night so there was not much in her stomach to come up. A viscous stream of bitter-tasting yellow-green bile trailed between the sink and her bottom lip. She spat disgustedly to get rid of it. But it clung on and finally she had to wipe it free from her mouth with a finger and scrape it off. Another involuntary vomit spasm wracked her throat painfully but nothing came up. Kate put her head low between her knees and moaned in abject misery. Jill, the black Labrador, sat in front of her. She put up a paw and whined in maternal sympathy. Kate looked up, her eyes streaming with tears, and let the paw lie in the palm of her hand.

'Here's to motherhood,' she said, just managing to finish the sentence before another empty spasm made her jerk her head over the sink.

Sally went to answer the door when the bell rang, holding the excitable Number Five by the collar to restrain her. There was a young man standing on the step. The quilted anorak he wore made him look disproportionately fat but Sally could see from his face that he was actually quite slim and athletic. His eyes were a distinctive shade of green, and there was a healed four-inch scar on the line of his jaw. He had shaved that morning but missed a bit beside his right ear. The stranger removed his black woollen hat in a curiously old-fashioned gesture of respect.

'Hello,' he said. 'I'm Philip.'

Sally arched her eyebrows, waiting for a further explanation but beginning to intuitively understand.

'Philip Grant. I'm Kate's friend.'

'Are you now? You'd better come in then.'

In the sitting room Grant proved to be as small and slim as she had thought when shorn of his outdoor clothing. Number Five sat on the floor guarding him. He sat on the edge of the sofa, fidgeting nervously while making polite conversation about the weather and his journey north. Sally fetched coffee and biscuits, knocking on the bathroom door as she passed.

'How long have you known Kate?' Sally asked, pretending she had no idea what was going on.

'Not long. Since the beginning of the year maybe.'

'You live in London then?'

'Yes. I'm from Edinburgh originally though. I'm hoping to come back soon.'

He made his return sound like a qualification she should be impressed by. He began to explain what he did for a living, something to do with finance and insurance, and his ambitions to start his own company. She let him ramble on but then felt sorry for him when he ran out of words and an awkward silence developed.

'So you know Kate?'

'Yes.'

Jill came into the room first and went straight to the stranger to sniff his hands. Number Five growled to show that she had the situation under control. Kate entered next, shuffling along, looking terribly ill with her chalk-white skin and hair hanging in greasy rats' tails. Sally saw surprise register on her face, quickly followed by indications of relief and pleasure. She was suddenly reinvigorated and healthy. A blush ran over her skin, reddening her neck most. Her eyes sparkled. Grant stood up in welcome. Sally looked from one to the other.

'Philip has come to visit you,' she said.

'Hello, Kate,' Grant said.

'Hello, Philip,' Kate replied.

'He's a friend of yours from London,' Sally said unnecessarily.

'Yes, I know.'

'It's good to see you, Kate.'

121

'It's good to see you, Philip. I didn't think you'd bother to come.'

'Don't be silly. I drove all night to get here.'

'Did you?'

'Once I realized you were gone.'

'So he's a friend of yours,' Sally said, filling in the pauses when they just stared at each other meaningfully.

'He is, but he's something more too, Mum.'

'Is he? What's that?'

'He's also the father of my unborn baby.'

It was Grant's turn to look surprised, shocked even. Sally nodded sagely, patting Jill's head, showing no outward reaction. Kate hadn't told him before. She had waited until he came looking for her. It was the kind of thing Sally would have done herself, just to be sure he was the right man for her. She watched a delightfully childish smile form on her daughter's lips and turned to admire the handsome face of the unexpected visitor. He would be married, of course. A minor problem.

'Isn't that nice,' Sally said.

35

Thursday: 10.57

David Fyfe and Connor Harper were led along twisting corridors, through archways and fire doors, and up and down contradictory flights of stairs and finally ushered into Professor Grant McDougall's top-floor office at the university's medical school. The window looked out onto the tops of trees in the big inner-city open space called the Meadows and across to the chaotic collection of architectural styles that made up the old Royal Infirmary, from ornate Victorian Gothic to functional flat-roofed steel and glass blocks. The urgency of an ambulance siren was fading as McDougall rose from the seat behind his desk to greet them. His smile was so wide his teeth showed through the undergrowth of his beard.

'Gentlemen, gentlemen,' he enthused, spilling tobacco from his smouldering pipe onto the papers in front of him. 'I hope what we are about to tell you will assist in your inquiries. It is a strange story and an intriguing one as I'm sure you will agree once you have heard it. Let me introduce you to Professor Neil Fleming from our social anthropology department.'

Fyfe turned to Fleming, who was standing in the corner, and removed his dark glasses. They shook hands and no mention was made of the fading bruises on Fyfe's face. Fleming was a wide-shouldered man with a big bald head that seemed too heavy for his neck, and a childishly earnest expression. His handshake was limp and he did not so much smile as grimace. Harper acknowledged him from beside the door. The office with its wallcharts, bookshelves and antique, leather-topped desk was too small for four full-grown men. They were all invading each other's space and did not want to move around unnecessarily. A pigeon flapped at the window, bumping against the glass, catching everyone's attention as it momentarily spread-eagled itself like a drawing on a coat of arms, then vanished.

'Anthropology? Is that a science?' Fyfe asked.

'It is the science of the human being in the widest sense, the study of mankind in relation to his environment,' Fleming said.

'Right, I see.'

'It's very popular with students in the faculty as a study option.'

Fyfe and Harper exchanged glances of professionally amused tolerance, excusing the eccentricity of academics in their ivory towers. Fyfe leaned against the edge of the desk, suddenly aware of how tired he was and wondering what an aspiring anthropologist would make of his dabbling in deliberate violence and devious adultery over the last few days. Connor Harper's erratic behaviour would also interest a scientifically trained mind. The pair of them could hire themselves out as study options. Maybe they could earn a decent living at it.

'We play golf together,' McDougall was saying. 'We're both members at Luffness. That's where we made the breakthrough.'

'Really? At Luffness? I've played there, not very well but I've played there. Knocked a few tiles off the clubhouse roof,' Fyfe interjected.

'It was at the seventeenth yesterday,' Fleming said. 'It was a pretty miserable day and Grant had been talking about the poison deaths and, of course, I had read about them in the papers. I was waiting to putt when I realized a possible solution to your puzzle.'

'Yes he did,' McDougall interrupted. 'I spent most of last night checking and it looks like we have a positive result.'

'It was the rain,' Fleming added. 'It was running down my neck when I was sheltering behind some bushes, reminded me of the rainforest. That's when it came to me.'

Fyfe looked from one to the other and wondered if he should take out his notebook to record the revelation. He decided against it. He could not imagine the Luffness course out on the wind-blasted East Lothian coast reminding anyone of sound mind of a tropical rainforest. There was not a tree to be seen, only the occasional clump of wind-shaped and stunted gorse bushes. On the way over Harper had warned him that McDougall was a little other-worldly in his blackened sandstone tower here at the university. McDougall's colleague did not disappoint on that front either.

'Frogs,' Fleming said, frowning to emphasize his seriousness.

'Frogs?' Fyfe repeated.

'South American frogs.'

'South American frogs?'

'Phyllobates terribilis to be exact, found only in a small area of lowland rainforest in western Colombia. They are one of a species otherwise known collectively as poison dart frogs because the natives, the Embaro Choco, use the toxic secretions to tip their blowpipe darts. Two inches long they are, bright yellow with a green cast, and lethal to the touch.'

'Two inches long,' Fyfe said. 'The frogs or the natives?'

'The frogs, of course.'

'Killer frogs? Is that what we've got then?'

'Professor McDougall has confirmed that the unidentified toxin found in the blood of all these unfortunate people comes from this source,' Fleming replied.

McDougall was standing by the small white marble fireplace with its empty grate. He had one foot on the fender and one arm stretched along the mantelpiece. He puffed languidly at his refilled pipe and stroked his beard as if it was his dog. He confirmed Fleming's statement with a slow and self-important nod.

'It is a very rare poison and an extremely powerful one,' he explained. 'It is one of the most potent toxins known. I would have identified it eventually but it could have taken months without Professor Fleming's intervention. Once I knew where to look it was simple. Lucky we decided to play golf really. We almost called the game off. It was threatening to rain.'

'I did field research in Colombia myself as a young anthropologist,' Fleming said. 'That was how I knew. When I heard about the hallucinations and zombie-like behaviour it seemed to fit perfectly. The Embaro Choco feared terribilis more than any other poison frog. It causes heart failure, usually within twenty-four hours. The heart just seizes up as the muscles harden if victims don't kill themselves first from the hallucinatory effect. I saw a woman die after accidentally treading on a terribilis. If it had been any other kind they might have been able to help her but because it was a yellow terribilis nobody would touch her. They said the frog's tongue was waiting in every skin pore for the next victim. They followed her out of the village and just stood and watched as she jumped off a cliff.'

'If they had touched her they could have been contaminated,' McDougall said. 'Once the poison is in the blood there is an end stage when the victim is as lethal to touch as the frog itself because the poison is in their sweat. A microscopic amount can be fatal to a human.'

Fyfe remembered the dead train cleaner and Davidson's head hurtling at him, knocking him unconscious. He didn't ask for more details. No one had suggested he was at risk but that didn't mean he wasn't. At least he hadn't given mouth to mouth. That would have been a death sentence. Fyfe thought of the city map with the apparently random locations where the victims had been found. The chain of circumstance was beginning to make sense. The two dead girls and the dog which must have been in contact with one girl before she died. The dog bites its master having earlier licked the hand of the bus driver in the street. He imagined a little yellow frog hopping from one to another and hoped it wasn't a sign that he was beginning to hallucinate.

125

'Killer frogs. That's what we've got.'

Fyfe took out his notebook and had the frog's Latin name spelled out for him. He jotted down other facts that the two professors threw at him; the range of poison dart frogs across Brazil, Venezuela, Ecuador, Peru and Colombia, that despite the generic name only fifty-five out of 135 different species were truly poisonous and only three species had a poison strong enough for hunters to use on their darts. The compounds secreted by the frogs were in the same class of chemicals as morphine and cocaine, but were many hundreds of times more powerful. Pharmaceutical companies were working on finding a commercial use for some of them. The toxin would affect human beings differently, depending on height-weight ratio and metabolic rates. Frogs secreted the poison continually as it seemed to evaporate within about thirty minutes of contact with air. So dead frogs were not hazardous and they did not leave a trail of poison that might kill anything following behind. Only living specimens were capable of killing.

Fleming produced a colour photograph of a Phyllobates terribilis from his inside pocket. Fyfe held the picture by a corner and looked into the bulging black eyes of the tiny beast that stared back at him from a vegetation-littered forest floor. The frog was bright yellow but its mouth was a green line and there were patches of light green on its stomach and sides. Its three-toed legs had what looked like black fingernail polish on the tips.

'Killer frogs,' Fyfe said again. 'Why is it such a garish colour?'

'It's a warning to predators to leave it alone. The brighter the better in evolutionary terms.'

'What happens if a predator ignores the warning?'

'It can only do so once and then it's dead. Birds and tarantula which prey on tree frogs have a genetic memory that makes the warning extremely effective. Nothing messes with Phyllobates terribilis.'

'I see, and how would these frogs get over here from the rainforest?'

McDougall shrugged. 'There are collectors who covet such things but because the frogs are so rare live exports are banned. No zoos in this country have any Phyllobates terribilis, I checked. Other species are fairly common in reptile and amphibian houses. Most are benign of course because it has proved impossible to breed poison producers in captivity. Any offspring are the same colour but never toxic for reasons we don't really understand. It's the diet probably.'

'Thanks for this. It's most helpful.'

'I told you it was fascinating. What will you do now?'

'Try to find where these frogs are and what happened to start this process.'

Fleming cleared his throat to announce that he was about to speak. *'Cherchez le grenouille,'* he said, patting his bald head self-consciously and blushing a bit when nobody laughed.

'Yes, something like that.'

Fyfe could now see the potential link between the two groupings of poison victims. Belinda Struthers had been found a few streets away from Scott Anderson and the report said his dead dog had habitually roamed the streets during the day. So it might have found Belinda dying, then Billy Stoddart in passing before the devils got into its head and made it go mad. There was still no obvious explanation for Belinda or Virginia Stevenson, the fallen angel at the cemetery, or Davidson, all of whom had been poisoned originally. It looked possible that there had been no murders at all, just a rather unfortunate accident in the first instance and then a chain of consequences by close contact. The blue movies with Davidson and the girls were just an entertaining diversion for investigators aiming in the wrong direction. Then again, somebody had to take the blame. They might discover that multinational companies were smuggling the frogs into the country for illicit experiments at secret laboratories to create new wonder drugs. Maybe animal liberationists had liberated a few and even now they were surrounding the city.

Fyfe thanked the two professors, shook hands, told them somebody would come round to take formal statements, replaced his dark glasses and turned to push Harper ahead of him out of the door. They walked in reflective silence until they had reached the ground floor and were buttoning up their coats before going outside. Fyfe held up the photograph of the frog for another look.

'What do you make of all that then?'

'Unexpected,' Harper said. 'Adds a little colour to our inquiries.'

'How do you think our lurid little pal got here?'

'Maybe someone brought the yellow monster over from Colombia and didn't keep the lid on the box properly.'

'It's a possibility.'

'Or maybe he did keep it in a box so that he could use it to tip his blowpipe darts before going out to shoot young girls and bus drivers.'

'The concept of a frog as a murder weapon is quite exotic, don't you think?' Fyfe said.

'Stranger things have happened, I suppose,' Harper replied. 'Not that I can think of any at the moment.'

36

Thursday: 13.48

Sally Fyfe hurried to answer the door when the bell rang. Jill and Number Five followed her. She had got through a frenzy of house cleaning since Kate and her lover had gone out for lunch together so they could be alone. Every room had been done, every ornament, picture frame and flat surface dusted. The bath and the toilet sparkled. The kitchen floor shone. The house was in perfect shape.

She had not heard the car on the gravel driveway but that would be Kate and Philip returning now, she thought as she ran down the stairs, hopefully to announce they were a couple once more. She was glad. She believed she had always known Kate's husband Doug, violent bastard that he was, could not have been the father of her only daughter's baby. She had never really liked him, having caught him raking through the drawers of Kate's bedroom soon after they became serious. She had never told Kate about that. If she had, the wedding might never have happened. Too late now, she murmured to herself. It was not useful to dwell on it. It needed to be fixed in the past so Kate could start all over again. She sensed that this Philip Grant was a different proposition, and she was looking forward to being a grandmother.

She had shifted the coat-stand and the untidy pile of wellingtons and old shoes while she was hoovering the hall carpet so that they blocked the back of the door. She had to move the stuff out of the way. The dogs sat down and waited. The bell rang impatiently twice more before she was ready to open the door. She paused, straightened her hair, checked in the mirror that her lipstick had not stained her teeth, wished she had sprayed some anti-perspirant under her arms. The bell rang again. She pulled the door open. The welcoming smile froze on her face and her spine felt as if a block of ice had been pressed against it.

'Hello, Mother,' Doug said. 'Long time no see.'

The dogs growled threateningly. Doug looked terrible. His hair was wild and unkempt. Both eyes were bloodshot in a chalk-white face dirtied on the jawline by dark stubble. His breathing rasped painfully. His left arm was in a sling underneath his leather jacket. There was a thin plaster cast on his lower left leg, showing through the split denim of his jeans. He limped forward a step and grunted with pain. Sally could not look away from the square-barrelled gun he held in his right hand, pointing at her stomach.

'Well Mother, aren't you going to invite your favourite son-in-law inside?'

37

Thursday: 15.26

David Fyfe and Connor Harper were about to get out of the car when the geese swarmed out of the long grass and came waddling towards them with their necks straining, wings spread, honking threateningly. The men shut the doors and stayed inside the car which was quickly surrounded by the grey and white geese. Beaks bumped against the metal. Some of the bigger birds had necks long enough to be able to reach the windows and tap at the glass. There must have been almost fifty in the flock. The car was completely encircled. Fyfe tried to sound the horn but couldn't find it. They had taken a pool car from the headquarters' fleet and neither of them were familiar with the controls. A search around the steering wheel eventually found the stalk required. A first blast, a magnified electronic version of their own honking, startled the birds and made them retreat several yards. Fyfe kept blasting the horn hoping it would drive them away but the geese were quick learners and when they realized there was no danger associated with the noise, returned to their aggressive stances around the car bumping threateningly against the metal.

Fyfe's mobile phone buzzed. He answered it and heard a voice in his ear that he did not recognize for a few seconds. Then he remembered the black policewoman's face materializing above him as he regained consciousness in the London hospital after being attacked. It brought back the throbbing headache. He pinched the bridge of his nose between finger and thumb and massaged the spot softly.

'I've got some information to pass on to you, sir,' Joan said.

'Go on then.'

'We've found Bruce Davidson.'

'Where?'

'On a mudflat at the side of the Thames below Hammersmith Bridge.'

Fyfe stared a bold goose in the eye. 'Dead, I take it?'

'Oh yes, sir. Very dead.'

'Suicide.'

'It looks like drowning so suicide, yes.'

'Thanks, Joan.'

'How's the head?'

'Still buzzing.' He sounded the horn again.

'See you the next time you're down in the deep south.'

'Rely on it.'

'You'll be coming back to finish your course?'

'One of these days probably. Bye now.'

An old man in a knee-length apron emerged from the door and walked round the side of a small van with a broken brake light and a bumper tied on with green binder twine. He shooed the birds away. They went obediently, waggling their little tufty tails, slowly disappearing into their hiding places in the long grass.

Fyfe got out of the car and introduced himself as a detective to the man, explaining that they were investigating the deaths of four people, thinking that it was five people even as he said it, and watched the man nod when asked if he was Michael Guthrie. Fyfe observed him carefully. His first impression was that the man was decently surprised. He didn't overreact, nor did he go to the opposite extreme and pretend it was an everyday thing to be questioned in the course of a murder investigation. It was his manner that conveyed his attitude. The wide moustache that hid his mouth made his whole face seem blank and expressionless. Harper came forward and showed his identity card. Fyfe was suddenly anxious to get the formalities over and done with. Guthrie had been singled out from a list of animal breeders in the Yellow Pages. One of only four registered businesses in and around the city once dogs and cats were excluded. The addresses were divided up among the squad. Fyfe got first choice. Guthrie's place behind the screen of trees on the south side of the bypass was on Fyfe's route home and they were halfway there before Fyfe realized that, for all his careful planning, he would have to double back again to drop Harper off once they finished the interview. As Harper's self-appointed counsellor and spiritual guide, he couldn't leave the job half done.

'Better than a burglar alarm,' Harper said, waving over at the retreating geese.

'They do tend to keep unwanted visitors away,' Guthrie acknowledged. 'They wouldn't hurt you though. If you stand up to them they turn and run. How can I help you, gentlemen?'

'You supply a number of pet shops, we understand?'

'That's correct.'

'Reptiles and snakes and stuff like that.'

'Parrots, parakeets, reptiles, amphibians. I used to do smaller mammals like monkeys but gave that up a few years ago. Birds and reptiles are much easier. Birds are the most profitable.'

131

Fyfe remembered the snapshot of Bruce Davidson with the parakeet on his shoulder. That reminded him of the videos he had brought back from London and that they were still in the holdall he had left at Harper's flat. He would collect the bag and view the videos once he got home to see if they contained anything relevant. The technician still hadn't got round to repairing the equipment in the clarty room at head-quarters.

'Frogs?'

'Yes. Any kind you want. They are very popular.'

'How about a Phyllobates terribilis?'

'Okay then, maybe not any kind. That's an extremely rare species. I don't think I've ever seen one except in books.'

If there was any hesitation in Guthrie's voice or manner, Fyfe couldn't make it out. The expressionless face stared back at him. The hairs of the moustache rippled and Fyfe thought of small animals running through the undergrowth of the graveyard where the first girl's body had been found. He shivered and self-consciously touched his tender nose, picturing Bruce Davidson jumping off a bridge and subsequently being washed up on some filthy mudflat at low tide.

'You wouldn't happen to breed the frogs here then?'

Guthrie shook his head. 'I do frogs but Phyllobates terribilis would be impossible. Poison dart frogs are notoriously difficult to breed in captivity. Terribilis, I am sure, would be more diffi-cult than most.'

'You do know about them then?'

'Only in an academic sense. I doubt if many pet shops would be interested in taking them.'

'You are aware that they are lethally poisonous?'

'That's why the pet shops wouldn't take them.'

'Of course. What about collectors?'

'There is a market in frogs, I suppose, but it is very specialized, a sub-division of mainstream herpetology.'

'Herpetology? Is that infectious?'

'The study of reptiles,' Guthrie said. 'I am a commercial breeder; it wouldn't be worth my while to bother with such rare exotica. I've done orange-toed lizards but they're hardly cost effective. I don't even think the zoo has any terribilis.'

'It doesn't. The zoo says the nearest ones it knows of are in Japan.'

'Or South America. That's where they originate. A small patch of lowland rainforest in Colombia is, I think, their only known breeding ground.'

'You know quite a lot about our little yellow chums.'

'I do. It's a fascinating subject.'

'Fascinating,' Fyfe agreed.

Guthrie's eyes narrowed. 'You're not going to tell me these deaths I've read about in the papers are being blamed on poison from Phyllobates terribilis?'

'No, I'm not going to tell you that.'

'It's not believable.'

'Isn't it?'

Guthrie shook his head and put his hands into the front pocket of his apron as if he was searching for something. A goose honked loudly and the raucous cry of a parrot came from inside. Fyfe caught a surreptitious glimpse of his watch and thought he smelled something burning.

'They couldn't survive anywhere around here, could they?' Fyfe looked over to the long grass hiding the geese. 'I don't mean here specifically. I mean they couldn't have escaped from somewhere accidentally and started breeding by themselves.'

'Our climate is far too cold. Tropical frogs wouldn't last for long in the open here. If there are any terribilis around they would have to be pampered and kept in strictly temperature-controlled conditions.'

'You have such conditions?'

'I do but I keep mostly harmless things.'

'And belligerent geese.'

'Them as well. I used to do alligators when I was running my shops but not any more. This is my business now. Let me show you.'

Guthrie led them inside, taking them on a tour of the bird-house full of colourful and noisy parrots. Then the aquarium-style tanks occupied by various lizards and snakes and other wriggling and scampering beasts. Both Fyfe and Harper stepped back as he picked out a young Burmese python as thick as his arm, draped it over his shoulder and lovingly stroked its small head. It seemed to be studying them as its tongue flickered menacingly. Fyfe didn't know if pythons were poisonous or if their trick was to squeeze the life out of their victims.

'Without me,' Guthrie said, 'all these birds and animals would never have lived. They would simply never have existed.'

'You consider yourself a god then?'

'Within my own specific boundaries, a kind of god if you like, yes.'

There was a pause as this information was absorbed. Fyfe glanced at Harper to share the unspoken belief that Michael Guthrie was, if not totally barking mad, at the very least endearingly eccentric. Fyfe thought back to the time when his black Labrador Jill gave birth to her litter of pups, tiny blind bundles of warm fur, Number Five the smallest of the lot. The new-born pups were both inconsequential scraps of life and incredibly complex biological organisms that were sophisticated far beyond anything human science could manufacture. Then he thought of the stone angel embedded face first in the ground and Virginia's dead body alongside it, the other dead girl sitting with her back against the wall, and the baby currently growing inside his daughter's womb: all of them, every last one of them, apparently inconsequential scraps of life.

Guthrie replaced the python in its tank and opened a plastic box on a shelf above it. He took out a dead rat and dropped it in beside the snake. Guthrie's neck appeared to have sunk down so far that his head was balanced directly on his upper chest. He stood in front of Fyfe and Harper and wiped his hands on the apron. Then he clasped them lightly together as if he was holding something small and delicate between the palms.

'Do you read the Bible, Chief Inspector?'

'Not regularly,' Fyfe replied.

'I do. Very regularly. I never tire of it but I haven't been inside a church for thirty years.'

'Loss of faith?'

'Gain of wisdom I would call it. I read the Bible though.'

'But you're not religious.'

Guthrie nodded. 'You should read it, too. It's all there.'

'All what?'

'All. Everything.'

'What do you mean? Everything about snakes and frogs?'

'I'm there,' Guthrie said without a pause. 'You're there. Inspector Harper is there. We're all there. The whole world.'

'Are we? What's it say about you?'

'About me?'

'Yes. You.'

Guthrie held out his hands still clasped together in an attitude of supplication. Fyfe fought an insistent urge to turn and run, expecting that the crazy old man in front of him was suddenly going to fling a deadly yellow frog at his face.

'The fool foldeth his hands together and eateth his own flesh,' Guthrie quoted, smiling curiously. 'He that is a fool walketh by the way, his wisdom faileth him and he saith to everyone that he is a fool.'

'Well, thank you very much for your time, Mr Guthrie,' Fyfe said. 'It's been most interesting.'

'We are all fools, Chief Inspector.'

'I can't argue with you on that one.'

Fyfe took Harper by the arm and led him away. Behind them Guthrie opened his hands to reveal that they were empty. His moustache bristled as the mouth underneath spread in a smile.

'All fools,' he shouted after them. 'All of us.'

38

Thursday: 15.32

Kate Fyfe was exhilarated. Her cheeks burned with the warmth of suffused blood. She and Philip had not gone out for lunch as they had said; instead they had walked on the Pentland Hills, following a footpath until they came to a wooden picnic table already carved with the initials of lovers who had passed the same way before them. Philip had taken his Swiss army knife and cut out a beautifully shaped heart to contain their names. Then he kissed her. Life was suddenly worth living again.

She pushed open the front door and pulled Philip, the father of her unborn child, after her as she ran along the hall. It had all worked out so well. She had dumped the abusive, unpredictable husband and the lover she had also abandoned had come looking for her to declare his unconditional love and explain just how much he wanted to get divorced and spend the rest of his life with her. That pledge was now carved into the weathered plank of an ancient picnic table for all to see. She had wept and he had wiped away the tears. It really was as corny as that.

Now she couldn't wait to tell her mother the good news, eager as a love-struck teenager to show off a new boyfriend. She burst into the living room and saw her mother sitting on the sofa. Jill was beside her and Number Five was at her feet. Both dogs looked round but neither moved. Number Five gave out a pathetic little yelp of recognition. Her mother looked round too, clinging tightly to the dogs' collars, and Kate was shocked by the tear tracks that ran like scars from her eyes down the sides of her nose and round her mouth. Even as she was about to ask what the matter was she noticed the figure slumped in the corner of the room, supported by the junction of the walls, with the plaster cast leg stretched out and an arm in a sling. The gun too, its ugly barrel pointing slightly downwards as though it was inordinately heavy and difficult to hold upright.

'Hello, darling,' her husband said. 'Welcome to our little gathering. Please take a seat, why don't you?'

He was unshaven and his eyelids were hooded. She raised a hand to her own fading bruises in unconscious empathy with his pain. The other hand covered her stomach and the invisible baby inside. In his torn and creased clothes, Doug resembled a drunk lying on a street corner, but a dangerous drunk with a gun, someone who could not be ignored. They stared at each other for several speechless, motionless seconds. Kate felt repressed anger leak like acid into her thoughts. He held her gaze, betraying no emotion. When Kate remained rooted to the spot in the doorway where she had stopped, mid-step, he waved the gun barrel impatiently, signalling to her to sit down. Behind her she felt

Philip's hands in the small of her back reassuring her that he was still with her. Doug didn't know that Philip was her new lover and the father of the baby growing inside her. He didn't even know she was pregnant. If she told him now it might change his attitude. Or it might make it worse. He was totally unpredictable. That was why she had run away from him originally. Anger was replaced by a strong instinct for self-preservation.

'Who's your friend?' Doug asked with mock politeness and an artificial smile that ended as a sneer.

'Nobody you know,' she replied slowly, regretting the sarcasm as soon as the words were out of her mouth.

He didn't seem to notice. 'You must introduce me then,' he said.

She stood aside and Grant stepped up to stand protectively by her side. 'Douglas Renwick,' she said, 'meet Philip Grant.'

'Good afternoon, Philip.' He passed the gun to his injured hand and pretended to offer a handshake before snatching his hand away at the last moment. The sneer widened. 'Welcome to the family, Philip. Do sit down and join us.'

They took seats directly opposite Sally and the dogs. Jill's lip was curled to expose the perfect curve of a pure white incisor tooth. The rumble of her low growl was just audible and no more.

'There now,' Doug said, wincing at some internal stab of pain. 'Happy families. Isn't this pleasant.'

39

Thursday: 17.18

Connor Harper flashed his headlights at a taxi on the way back into the city after visiting Guthrie. It stopped and Fyfe got into it. Harper watched it drive away, a hanging tail of vapour from the exhaust whipping and twisting in the cab's slipstream. He wished that he, too, was going back to a warm home and a welcoming family, a comfortable fireside and the willing embrace of a loving woman. Instead, he went on by himself to an empty flat, having been long ago abandoned by a vindictive wife and recently spurned by a hard-hearted mistress. At the entrance, he hung his head and sighed with conscious self-pity. He intended to get something to eat and then go back into the incident room to see if anything useful had come from the afternoon's work. At least Fyfe retained enough confidence in him to believe that he wouldn't just go and get drunk to blot everything out and forget about having to wake up in the morning to face another day. More fool Fyfe. What had the daft old man Guthrie said? We are all fools. Every one of us. Not far off the mark. Not far at all.

Harper thought of Sarah Smith, if that was her real name, and how the sallow-skinned waif had vanished into the night while they were searching Bruce Davidson's bolt-hole in the city. What future did she have? None at all. She was as good as dead, careering down a fatal slippery slope that started with her being filmed, still relatively hale and hearty, as she cavorted in Davidson's blue movies, his trademark stamped on her buttock. That flicker of memory reminded Harper of the holdall with the unseen video tapes Fyfe had brought back from London. Fyfe had mentioned it earlier but must have forgotten again. It was lying in his flat when the videos in it should have been at headquarters with the others to be examined for any value as evidence once the repair technician got his finger out. Sarah might appear on them as well, though he couldn't think of any more sexual acts that he hadn't already seen her performing on the videos.

He kept sighing as he sorted out his door keys. When his flat door swung open he was left standing with his hand raised to shoulder level and the key pointing forward, frozen with surprise at the unexpected sight of his young girlfriend Kelly directly in front of him. She was wearing nothing but a shirt, the one with Marilyn Monroe faces all over it that had been his everyday wear on holiday in Greece. She had one foot in front of the other and was up on her toes, poised precariously as if she was balanced on a tightrope. The atmosphere around her was thick and smoky. The air contained the unmistakably sweet smell of cannabis. All the curtains were drawn, concentrating the darkness. Kelly reached out her arms towards him, swayed a little, then came to greet him, moving as if she was underwater and colliding just as he pushed the door shut. Her arms went round his neck, her legs wrapped themselves round his thighs and she lifted herself off the floor to cling on tight.

'Where on earth have you been, lover boy?' she slurred. 'I've been waiting all day for you.'

She had been drinking too. He could taste the alcohol as she kissed him repeatedly, forcing open his mouth. He put his hands under her backside to hold her up and prevent them both falling over. The shirt flapped open, displaying her breasts and the delicately outlined muscle tone of her skin.

'I've come to say I'm sorry, darling. I'm really sorry for being so bad-tempered and treating you so nastily. Can you forgive me? Please. Please say you forgive me.'

Kelly pouted theatrically, fluttering her eyelashes. Harper delayed as long as he dared, then said, 'I forgive you.'

'I know I've been really nasty to you,' Kelly said between kisses. 'We have to make up. I've been waiting such a long time. Let's make up. I'm feeling incredibly horny.'

It was not the time for words, Harper realized. Nor was it the time for self-congratulation that she had given in before him. It was time for decisive action, certainly not time for going back to work. All self-pity and depressive tendencies abruptly banished, he began to stumble towards the bedroom before Kelly changed her mind.

40

Thursday: 18.39

Michael Guthrie stood at the door for ages after watching the policemen's car drive away down the track. The tyres kicked back some small stones. A few of the more determined geese followed it, honking defiantly. When it was finally out of sight

Guthrie doubled over and vomited onto the ground. A single convulsion sent the sour- tasting contents of his stomach rushing upwards, ballooning out his cheeks for a moment, and then pouring out of his mouth to land on the ground with a hollow-sounding splatter. All his strength seemed to be contained in the colourful stream of partly digested food now deposited at his feet and he had to hold onto the wall to stay upright. He spat to try and get rid of the taste and noticed that his legs were shaking uncontrollably. He knew they would be back. It was only a matter of time now that they had found him. The prospect terrified him. He started to weep and, because of the way his head was inclined, the tears ran across his cheeks and into his nostrils before dripping off the end of his nose.

He stayed doubled over by the door for a long time, gradually recovering from the nervous reaction that had caused him to be violently sick. He spat again and straightened up, feeling the strength in his legs return until he was able to let go of the wall with confidence. He stopped crying and wiped his eyes dry, bringing the familiar scenery with its backdrop of trees into focus. The police would be back, so he had to go. Both things seemed inevitable. The Bible stories were true then. He had denied them for so long that he thought he had shaken himself free. They had seemed such nice girls after all, so concerned about him, so understanding. Now he knew better but now he, too, was doomed. Galatians had the words for it. God is not mocked: for whatsoever a man soweth, that shall he also reap.

He remembered the fear he had seen so often reflected in the eyes of his cruel father, irrational fear that translated into inarticulate violent outbursts. Now he knew it had been fear of God. His sinful father had been right. There was a wrathful God to be afraid of and Guthrie, who had forsaken the church as a young embittered man, was afraid of him. It was as intimidatingly simple as that.

Guthrie went inside. In the birdhouse he began to crank the handle that turned the gearing mechanism that opened the three big skylights in the glass roof. Netting stretched automatically over the space that was created but he kept turning beyond the normal six turns. The mechanism was strong and well-oiled but began to tighten and more effort was needed to make the extra

140

turns. There was a creaking sound, the grating of metal on metal. He kept turning, forcing the reluctant handle round. The netting strained and tore with a loud ripping sound.

The parrots and the parakeets watched Guthrie curiously, heads cocked, as he opened all the doors of the various cages. A large flock of zebra finches were the first to take advantage of their unexpected freedom, spiralling once inside their ten-foot high cage, once inside the main part of the building, and then disappearing through one of the skylights like smoke up a chimney. A green and blue Amazonian parrot screeched an uncertain farewell and flew up to perch on the metal rafters.

Guthrie took the detachable iron handle and went through to the reptile house. He struck out at the first tank but the glass was too tough to break. It dented and clouded but the handle bounced off it, wrenching his shoulder painfully. He smashed another couple of tanks but then dropped the handle and began to pull the tanks over with his undamaged arm. They toppled onto the floor, bouncing and spilling their contents. Lizards scampered out, snakes slithered, frogs hopped for cover over the debris-strewn floor. Some birds flew through the open door, their flailing wings filling the air with confusion and a frantic sense of panic.

A small bird flew into Guthrie's face at the far end of the room. He swiped it away and stood, breathing heavily, beside the only tank he had not touched. Inside it he could see the bright yellow colours of a squad of small frogs half buried in the bedding of moss and tree bark. He reached in and scooped one out. The frog crouched motionless among the warm scraps of bedding littering the palm of his hand. Its black bulbous eyes stared, its wide green-tinged mouth seemed to grin menacingly at him. It made no attempt to move as he closed his fingers around it, forming a loose fist and then beginning to squeeze. The frog squirmed and tried to jump, but Guthrie held it fast in a tightening grip. Its bones cracked and it stopped moving. He felt a liquid coldness spread out over his hand, running between his fingers. He kept his fist tightly closed, raising it up in front of his face while the floor around his feet seemed to be moving with a fleeing tide of small animals. He pushed the fist into his mouth and, chewing at it with his lips, licked it dry. The taste was surprisingly pleasant.

41

Thursday: 18.51

Fyfe entered his living room and stopped dead. He took in the apparently harmless scene of Sally sitting with the dogs on one side, and Kate with a well-dressed stranger on the other, and straight in front his son-in-law's body on the floor, compressed uncomfortably into the angle of the walls.

'Hello, Dad,' Doug said. 'Now everyone's here.'

Fyfe frowned. The full details came to him only slowly. He saw the nervous expressions, the growling dogs held back by Sally. He saw the gun pointing at him and a flicker of fear made his heart lurch and caused him to breathe more rapidly. His first thought was that he was responsible for the situation because he had attacked Doug down in London and provoked him to this. Then he began to think that maybe he was hallucinating because the frog poison had been passed on to him by Bruce Davidson's head butt, the same Davidson who had drowned himself in the Thames as the poison seeped through his blood and affected his brain. So it was possible this wasn't actually happening. That it was all in Fyfe's mind. He was making it up. None of it was real. Not Sally's pleading, tear-stained glance. Not Kate's blank stare of fear. Not the battered body in plaster cast and sling lying in the corner threatening to shoot them all. None of it was real.

'We were discussing my illness, Dad. The doctors said I was ill, said I was a loony, said I was a schizophrenic. How we laughed, didn't we, Kate? They pumped me full of all sorts of drugs. I've had chlorpromazine, supiride, zuclopenthixol deconoate. I've had tablets. I've had injections. I've been detained in hospital against my will, but it's made no difference. You know why it's made no difference?'

He waited for a reply, looking round the room, finally fixing on Kate who quickly shook her head to appease him. Fyfe continued standing where he was, wondering if it would be possible to dive on top of Doug and smother the gun, to take the single bullet and save the others and become a martyr. If it was a hallucination he wouldn't really die anyway.

'I'm not ill, you see. Am I, Kate? I'm not ill at all. I'm a victim, but the doctors wouldn't believe me. Well, they will have to believe me now, won't they? Look at the state of me, for goodness' sake. Look at me. Don't tell me I made this up. I was attacked. They tried to kill me. They really did. They knocked down my door and tried to kill me. Look at me.'

'Who did?' Fyfe asked, worried that his voice would break with anxiety.

'The government. The government tried to kill me. They had masks on and they beat me with iron bars. They cut off my legs before but the doctors re-attached them. They poked out my eyes once but I found them under the bed. Then they came for me in my home. I had already sent Kate away because I knew they were coming. I'm glad I did that to keep her safe. They would have killed her too, you know. I was lucky. They will come for me again. They could come at any time. But don't worry, my darling, at least I can make sure that you will be safe.'

Doug smiled at Kate and she burst into tears. It would have been funny, Fyfe thought, if the situation was not so serious. He should have been at a seminar on hostage negotiating skills but instead he had triggered this bizarre episode by giving Doug reason to believe in his own fantasy. Now he was being held hostage and the eloquence of Doug's madness was truly terrifying. It was he, not Fyfe, who was hallucinating. He genuinely believed what he was saying. The pupils of his eyes stared out from his face like something hiding in the dark recesses of one of Guthrie's reptile tanks. It was all real enough to him, as substantial and as sinister as the gun he held in his hand. Whether they liked it or not, he was imposing his own version of reality on every other person in the room and they had to live within it. One man's hallucination was everybody else's nightmare.

'Why should the government want to kill you, Doug?' Fyfe asked.

'So that I won't testify against them, of course, Dad. You don't mind me calling you Dad do you, Dad? I know you never liked me but then fathers rarely like the men who take their daughters

143

from them. Its a Freudian thing apparently. Electra and Oedipus. One of my psychiatrists explained it all to me.'

'Did he?'

'Yes. They don't want me to give evidence because it would bring down the government. I know about the corruption in the sewers, you see. There would have to be a general election. It would be so inconvenient and the rats would have to be flushed down the toilet rather than buried in the garden to nourish the roots of the rowan trees.'

Doug spoke fluently and with the enthusiasm of an evangelical preacher. The illogicality of his language and the honest manner in which it was delivered was frightening. Both Sally and Kate were crying openly. Fyfe took a step forward but stopped as the gun was raised in response. We are all fools, Guthrie had said. How right he was.

'You're wondering why I've come here aren't you, Dad?'

Fyfe nodded, refusing to drop his gaze and look away, trying to see inside Doug's brain to be able to make an educated guess at what was going to happen next.

'They followed me but I fooled them. I left my car in the woods miles away and walked over the hill. It wasn't easy. Not with my leg like this. I made it though. Nobody knows I'm here. We're on our own.'

'Why are you here?'

'To make sure I won't be betrayed again.'

'Who betrayed you, Doug?'

'You know who betrayed me.'

Fyfe did know. He didn't call it betrayal, though, he called it payback time, but there seemed little value in arguing semantics with an armed and dangerous schizophrenic. Why did he have to get drunk in that pub and meet the helpful stranger? If he had just stayed in his hotel room and pulled the sheets over his head none of this would have happened. Now another stranger Fyfe didn't know was sitting on the edge of his chair beside Kate, looking as if he was about to leap on Doug given half a chance. Fyfe resented that. It was his house. It should be he who played the hero.

'No I don't,' Fyfe said. 'Tell me who betrayed you.'

Doug pushed with his uninjured right leg so that he sat a little

144

more upright in the corner. He made a circular motion with the gun and copied it with his head as if he was relieving stiffness in his neck.

'They're in this room,' he whispered. 'They followed me. They won't leave me alone.'

'Who is it?'

'I can't tell you or they'll cut out my tongue. They've done it before. They're watching me all the time. You have to guess.'

'Is it me?'

'No, it's not you. You're my friend.'

'Is it him?' Fyfe pointed to the stranger beside Kate.

'No, it's not him.'

'Is it Sally?'

'Such a nice name, Sally. I've always liked it. I fell in love with the name before we were introduced.'

Fyfe inched forward, ready to hurl himself between the gun and Kate. Doug raised his eyebrows, seeming to read his thoughts.

'Don't be silly,' Doug said. 'Kate would never betray me. We are very close. She has never hurt me. Why would she do such a thing?'

'Then who?'

Doug pushed himself upright, leaning awkwardly in the corner, making a dirty streak on the wallpaper. 'Ask yourself this. What colour is the Devil's helper?'

'I don't know.'

'The colour that blends with the night.'

'Grey? Black?'

'The colour of the hidden assassin.'

'Black?'

'So it must be.'

Fyfe saw that the gun barrel had swung round and was pointing directly at Sally. She closed her eyes. Jill, the black Labrador, had curled back her lip even more to expose a row of sharp white teeth. The sound of her growl heightened and she lunged forward. But Sally's fingers were hooked in her collar and she was held in mid-air, front paws scrabbling like a boxer squaring up for a fight. The birse had risen on Number Five's neck. She had her back arched like a spitting cat, growling in harmony.

Doug pushed himself off the wall to stand unaided. 'Die, you evil bitch,' he shouted hysterically. 'Die.'

Fyfe launched himself full-length and the gun swung round to point at him. He hit Doug hard in the stomach with his shoulder and slammed him against the wall. Kate's friend was right behind him, adding extra weight. The sound of the involuntary grunt as the breath was forced out of Doug's lungs was louder than the air-cushioned crack of the gun firing. Fyfe heard it in his left ear in mid-lunge and then the sequence of violent grunt, canine yelp, and high-pitched female scream. He wrenched the gun from Doug's limp hand and turned to see Sally, apparently uninjured, still on the sofa, still holding Jill by the collar. The dog was whining and writhing. Number Five was barking loudly.

'He shot the dog,' Sally said. 'He shot the dog. She's bleeding.'

There was a small but dramatic blob of bright scarlet on Jill's breast. It looked strangely artificial as the frightened dog tried to get her head as far away from it as possible, twisting Sally's wrist at the collar and breaking free. Fyfe grabbed her and got his arm round her neck to hold back her head and expose the wound. Number Five had broken free too but had stopped barking. Silence, except for Doug's painful attempts to gasp for air, descended on the room as Fyfe examined the wound that was masked by the black hairs, probing it tenderly to see just how bad it was. Using a finger and thumb as pincers, he picked the scarlet mark out and left Jill pristinely black once more. She began to lick at the hairs as he held up the piece of scarlet for the others to see, offering the gun with his other hand.

'It's a dart gun.' He laughed, feeling a twinge of sympathy and guilt at having assaulted Doug in the first place and provoked this confrontation. 'One of those things you fire at a fairground. Hardly powerful enough to dent the skin.'

Number Five went over to sniff at Jill. Sally put her arms round Fyfe and hugged him close, sobbing quietly. Kate did the same to the other man.

'He's mad,' she said, looking down at Doug where he lay. 'Completely mad.'

'There will be a Latin name for it but you're absolutely right,' Fyfe replied, all his anger dissipated. 'He must be suffering from some pretty serious mental illness.'

146

'Shall I call the police?' Kate's friend asked.

'Better to call a doctor,' Fyfe said, patting Jill's head and checking she was all right. There was no blood. She licked his hand. The rough texture of her tongue convinced him he was not in the middle of any hallucination. His main concern now that Doug was no longer a threat was to ensure that he was treated well. It wasn't, Fyfe thought uncomfortably, all his fault.

'Sally, have you got Dr Somerville's number? We can have him sectioned.'

'What does that mean?'

'They come, put a straitjacket on him, cart him away and lock him up.'

'Poor bastard.'

Fyfe looked down and Sally squeezed his hand. 'Believe me, it could happen to any of us,' he said, believing it himself.

42

Thursday: 19.20

Harper lit another joint rolled with the high-grade stuff from the pouch on the bedside table. There was a fine sheen of perspiration on his skin and a lightness in his mind reflected in the permanent grin he could not get off his face, even though the muscles around his mouth and in his cheeks were getting sore. It was so good to be back in favour and back in Kelly's bed. He was physically exhausted and mentally drained. He loved it. He didn't feel like talking. He didn't feel like doing much of anything. He felt like he was soaking in a pleasantly warm bath with just his nostrils above the water to allow him to breathe. The bedclothes were in a heap on the floor. Kelly lay beside him on the mattress, stretching herself like a cream-satiated cat, arms pushing out above her head, breasts flattening, nipples rising, spine curving. He sat cross-legged and sucked the soothing smoke into his lungs, imagining it being absorbed from there into his blood and from there into his flesh, building layers of

147

happiness and contentment one on top of the other. It was beautifully restful. He took another drag but this time held the smoke in his mouth. He leaned over and put his lips against Kelly's. When her lips parted, he blew the smoke gently inside. She breathed deeply, purred and grabbed hold of the headboard to stretch some more. She was smiling too. He would have to go soon. They were expecting him back at headquarters.

'Did you enjoy that then?' she asked.

'Which bit exactly?'

'The making up bit that has restored our relationship to its previous state.'

'That was particularly pleasurable.'

'We must do it more often.'

'What? Fall out or make up?'

'Both. It makes life interesting and you can't have one without the other. You never told me about your hobby, by the way.'

'You never asked. What hobby?'

'You know. Don't be shy. I'm very broadminded.'

Harper tried to focus his thoughts. He didn't know what Kelly was talking about. Was she trying to be clever. What hobby? Winding her up? Him being stupid and insensitive? Was it something to do with the flowers that she had thrown back in his face when he had tried to make up with her earlier, before the time was right? That must be it, he decided. It must be the flowers. She was referring to him as an amateur florist. The way he did it he would never get a job as an Interflora delivery man.

'You didn't like my flowers,' he said.

'Forget the flowers. Why did you think I was so horny when you arrived,' Kelly said, starting to stroke his arm. 'I'd been watching them all day waiting for you.'

'Watching who?'

'I didn't know what they were at first. I led a very sheltered life before I met you.' She nipped his arm and when he didn't respond nipped him harder, only stopping when he pretended to be in pain. 'I didn't think I would but I actually found it quite a turn-on.'

'What? Me?'

'I couldn't do it myself, of course. Not in front of anyone else but I like to watch. It was cool.'

'Cool,' Harper repeated dumbly.

'Yeah. Cool. I'm finding out all sorts of new things about myself.'

'It was cool,' Harper agreed.

Kelly scrambled to her knees in front of him, taking the last bit of the joint from his fingers and stubbing it out in the ashtray. The smile on her face was so wide he expected her lower jaw to drop off.

'Let's watch them together. Just you and me.'

'Sure thing, Kelly. Watch what?'

She was gone in a flurry of blurred flesh and flying hair, leaving Harper squatting on the bed still wondering what she was talking about. His grin slowly turned to a puzzled frown. He moved slowly, untangling his limbs and taking tentative steps as though the ground below his feet might be treacherous and uneven. He tripped twice before he reached the bedroom door but finally managed to get through it. Kelly was lying flat out on the sofa, leaning back on her elbows with her legs bent at the knee. The light from the big television screen gave her skin a strangely artificial glow. She made a big show of blowing him a kiss and waggled her legs in the air.

'Come and sit beside me. The show starts here.'

Kelly turned her face back to the screen. He sat down beside her and followed the direction of her look, watching the scene shift from the disc of a cold sun seen through tree branches against the sky, slowly down to tangled undergrowth and gravestones. The camera focused on a fallen statue of an angel embedded in the ground and then quickly drew back to reveal a woman standing behind it. She was wrapped in a huge army-style greatcoat and her hair hid her face. She titled her head back and spread her arms wide to open the coat. Underneath she was totally naked. The camera zoomed in on a name carved in moss-covered stone.

'Virginia,' Harper said.

'It gets better soon,' Kelly told him, shifting so that she could lie across his lap. 'Where do you get this kind of thing?'

The scene changed to an interior. A featureless room with a double bed and two naked women kneeling with their backs to the camera, mooning. They displayed identical tattoos like

149

bruises on their buttocks. Then they fell onto the mattress, one to the left and one to the right, to reveal the old man with the thick grey moustache who was lying under them.

Kelly squeezed Harper's testicles. 'Watch and learn, lover boy. I hope your heart is as strong as the old geezer on the screen. If it isn't you may not survive what is about to happen to you.'

43

Thursday: 20.45

Philip Grant shook hands and explained who he was, what he had done to Kate, and why he was there while Fyfe drove to the local GP's home with Doug tightly wrapped in an old dog blanket and pushed down into the space behind the front seats of the purple Volvo estate. The dogs were in the rear space behind the guard and Grant sat in the back seat with his feet on Doug to make sure he didn't suddenly rise up and cause more problems. Doug made no attempt to escape from his position. All he did was moan pathetically, occasionally breaking into lucid but incomprehensible outbursts explaining how he had learned to walk without legs after his enemies had cut them off and stored them in a waist-high stainless-steel jug. Fyfe persuaded Grant that it was not necessary to mention the dart gun. No point in kicking a man too hard when he was down.

Roger Somerville was a doctor of the old school, close to retirement with fly-away eyebrows and copious nostril hair framed by a ruddy, broken blood-vessel strewn face. He had been a regular police surgeon until a few years earlier when he decided he didn't need the hassle. Now he stuck to general practice, dishing out pills and tranquillizers to keep his flock of patients satisfied and sane, hopefully both. He had seen it all and nothing surprised him. He came to the door with a napkin tucked into the collar of his shirt, spaghetti sauce on his top lip and a balloon glass full of red wine in his hand. He listened patiently to Fyfe's story, not interrupting once. When it was finished he took a large swallow of wine and turned his head away to belch quietly. He came outside and nodded to Grant to move out of the way. He leaned into the back of the car, pulled back the blanket and shone a pencil torch into Doug's pupils. Doug obligingly told him about masked assailants and his legs being amputated as a demonstration of how mad he was. The doctor straightened up slowly, grimacing, with his hands pressed into his sides.

'We'd better get the bugger shut away then,' he announced.

Somerville got his coat and his doctor's bag and phoned the main psychiatric hospital in Edinburgh to warn them what was coming. He sat in the passenger seat and, ignoring the grunting from the rear, began a long involved tale about the last time he had been called out to section a schizophrenic and how it had taken him hours to coax the chap out from under his mother's bed. His delusion was that he was in imminent danger of being seized in the talons of a passing eagle and carried off to an eyrie on a mountainside somewhere. As Somerville led him through the living room with a caring arm around his shoulder, his mother's budgie, allowed the freedom to fly about the house, had fluttered across the hall and before anyone had a chance to stop him he had shot back under the bed.

'What happened then?' Grant asked from the back.

'We shut the bloody budgie in its cage, eventually got our man out from under the bed again, pumped him full of neuroleptics to calm him down and locked him up.'

'Is that what will happen to Doug?'

'Most probably. Medical science can do many wonderful things but it has yet to achieve a proper cure for people whose brains short-circuit.' He suddenly sat forward in his seat. 'What's that?'

He pointed off to the left, bumping the windscreen with his fingertip. The Volvo was fast approaching the outskirts of the city and the bypass which encircled it. Fyfe saw smoke rising above a barrier of trees. Crows drifted among it like swirling scraps of burned paper. A flickering blue cast to the glow of lights from beyond the trees added another surreal element to the scene. It was Guthrie's place and it was on fire.

Fyfe stopped the car at the side of the road and they all watched the smoke and the crows for a few minutes.

'I have to go,' Fyfe said. 'Can you drive on to the hospital and make all the arrangements?'

Somerville eyed him curiously. 'What's over there?' he asked.

'It's to do with a current investigation.'

'Those women that were poisoned?'

'Could be. I'm not sure. We talked to someone there a few hours ago.'

'Duty calls then. You'd better run along and find out what the score is. Don't worry. I'll organize everything.'

The dogs barked their annoyance at being left behind. Somerville slid awkwardly across into the driving seat of the big car as Fyfe climbed the fence and crossed the field to the trees. By the time he reached them and looked back the car had disappeared. On the other side of the trees, across a 200 yard wide patch of rough ground, he saw three fire engines and an ambulance and a confusion of flashing lights and flames leaping from the roof of the steading. This couldn't be coincidence, he thought. They should have taken Guthrie more seriously as a suspect when they first had him. Something flew past his head. In the darkness he assumed it to be a bat but it passed with an incongruous flash of colour. He waded into the long grass, remembering how this had all started with him walking away from the moss-covered fallen angel in the overgrown cemetery, invisible creatures scuttling to uncertain safety around him. He kept a look-out for the geese and hurried towards the fire.

44

Thursday: 20.48

Michael Guthrie felt the searing heat from the flames rubbing against his skin like rough sandpaper. The animals had fled. The cages and tanks were empty. He had stood and watched, like

Noah emptying the Ark on finding dry land after the flood. The birds and beasts ranged outwards to populate the new world that would have to exist without him in it.

He swallowed the hot air and it singed the lining of his throat. The heat roasted his lungs and was so severe his internal organs began to bubble and pop. He stood erect at the centre of a roaring cylinder of flame that was shrinking around him, working him like the muscles in a snake's stomach, consuming him, digesting him, slowly killing him. He sucked in a deep breath and a layer of his outer skin was incinerated. He became smaller, dwindling even as he looked down on his own body that smoked and burned and shed avalanches of grey ashes.

He thought of himself as a child growing up and saw the innocent boy grow into the pagan man. He remembered young Bruce's promise and the two girls who seduced him in the graveyard and flaunted their nakedness before him, tempting the dormant devil within him that he had spent a lifetime learning to ignore. They aroused his wickedness, leaving him no real choice. Sexual lust leered in an ugly parody of joy as the two girls touched him and coaxed him and corrupted him and damned him to the furthest reaches of hell.

Then there was Bruce Davidson, still speaking amiably, still asking to be trusted, still being reasonable. He had delivered on his promise, he explained patiently, and had come to demand the payment he was owed or the pictures would be shown elsewhere. Guthrie, embarrassment and shame making him unable to speak, saw his hand signing a cheque, and another, and another, until there was hardly anything left in the bank account it had taken him so long to build up. He saw Bruce return to demand more money and, at the same time, he saw the way out that God in his wisdom had already provided in the small scraps of moist jelly-like spawn he had found among the bits of vegetation in the corner of the special crates the South American parrots came in. It had somehow survived the long transatlantic journey and Guthrie had not really expected anything to happen when he slipped the alien find into warm water and waited. He had in his mind the childhood memory of the host of wriggling tadpoles scooped up from the water of the boating pond and, sure enough, eventually a few sluggish tadpoles appeared, tiger-

153

striped, black and yellow. Then they turned into tiny frogs which grew into miniature grinning yellow monsters. It took him weeks of research to discover what species had been sent to him, many months more to appreciate the significance. To understand why this particular species, such a rare species, had homed in on him. Phyllobates terribilis was lethal, but nonetheless would have been welcome on board Noah's Ark. It had been sent to him to be safeguarded for the future use Guthrie was to require of it. Although he was not aware of it at the time of first discovery, it was to be the answer to his prayers.

It was easy to extract the poison and to put it in the drinks which, polite to the end, he had offered Bruce and the girls when they came for that one final time to claim what they were owed. And, as the poison invaded their minds, he took them in his van to their favourite places and let them slip away into the darkness like drowning victims resigned to slipping below the surface of the water. He knew then, as their solid flesh melted into the rustling of the dark night, that it would be impossible for him to survive. All is vanity and vexation of the spirit, the Bible said so accurately. He was not destroying anything, not the shame, not the girls, not himself. He was not saving himself. There was no escape from the endless torment to come. Why is it that all the rivers run into the sea, yet the sea is not full?

Guthrie breathed deeply and around him the oxygen-rich flames roared in response. He was growing smaller, eaten away from the outside. His body was burning, his flesh was melting to expose the chalk-white bones that then began to crumble to dust. He reached out and touched cold stone. He felt the contours of a face and in his imagination he saw tiny human figures trapped in a flood that washed over the sides of the palm of a human hand. He saw that he was among them, being swept towards the edge. His heart was bursting. His blood was boiling. His life was ending.

From a great distance outside him came an unholy clamour of clashing sound. Before long none of his physical self would remain. His soul was being reducing to a small pyramidical pile of powdered ashes. And when that was all that was left of him he knew a cooling breeze would gently part the ring of flames and disperse the ashes. They would rise like a snake responding to a charmer's music and then they would be gone.

45

Thursday: 22.05

Connor Harper saw Fyfe approaching and went to meet him. Once Harper had been shown Guthrie in action on the video with the two dead girls and the vanished Sarah, he had left Kelly despite her tempting protests and jumped into the car to get back to the incident room. As soon as he got there news of the fire at Guthrie's address had him turning round, tyres squealing in the car park, siren wailing to get him through a set of traffic lights and to put him in suitable emergency mood. There was, of course, nothing he could do once he arrived other than stand just close enough to feel involved because the heat was scorching his face. The firemen couldn't do much either. The front door was broken down with an axe, splintering spectacularly. A pair of lumbering men in full breathing kit went inside to check if the building was occupied. Harper hadn't contacted Fyfe because he wanted to take all the credit for being smart enough to get there at such short notice.

'How did you know about this?' Harper asked. 'I was just about to phone you but I didn't want to disturb you before there was something to tell.'

'I happened to be passing,' Fyfe replied. 'Have they found Guthrie?'

'Not yet. If he's there,' Harper said.

Fyfe moved the hand he was using to shield his face and pointed to the ambulance where a stretcher was being lifted into the back by two paramedics. 'Then who's being loaded on board?'

'That was the first firemen on the scene,' Harper told him. 'One of those bloody geese charged at him.'

'You're joking?'

'No. Knocked him flying. Broke his leg. You're lucky they didn't turn on you.'

'I could have warned you about the geese.'

'The whole gaggle kept the firemen trapped inside their engine for ten minutes while the fire was getting a good hold and the reptiles were roasting.'

'Is that what that smell is?'

'Then someone had the bright idea of turning the hoses on them.'

That explained why three firemen were standing, hoses in hand, with their backs to the main event, spraying the long grass where the geese had retreated. From Fyfe's angle it looked as if the firemen were pissing on them.

'If it takes a whole brigade to get past the guardian geese this fire must be a homer,' Fyfe said.

'You reckon it's deliberate then?'

'What do you think?'

'I don't think, boss. I know.'

'What do you know?'

'Remember those video tapes you brought back from London and left at my flat? I couldn't sleep so I watched them. Guess what?'

'Guthrie with our dead girls.'

Harper nodded. 'From every conceivable angle, believe me. Who would have thought the old guy had it in him? What stamina. You have to admire him. Tough guy Davidson must have got his tattooed harem to seduce the poor old bastard, then stepped in to blackmail him once he had it all on video.'

Fyfe shook his head. 'Funny what some people worry about, isn't it? Who would have cared? Who would Davidson have sold the videos to?'

'Who knows? Whatever the state of the market, Guthrie decided he wasn't going to play their game, extracted some deadly poison from his handy specimens to put in their tea or something and then, as they start to hallucinate, dumps them back in the city well away from the scene of the crime and goes back home to his birds and beasts.'

'Until we turn up on his doorstep.'

'He bluffs us and as soon as we've gone, realizing it can only be a matter of time before we discover the truth, sets about going out in a blaze of glory. He would find something in the Bible as a precedent to show him the way.'

'So you reckon he's in there burned to a crisp, do you?'

'I'd bet on it. And it will round the inquiry off nicely, don't you think? A decent suicide will save us some paperwork at least.'

A rogue goose, honking furiously, came rushing out of the grass and a fireman only just got his hose jet on it in time to force it back. A thin yellow and black snake wriggled over the ground between Fyfe's feet, seeking shelter. He and Harper stepped out of the way. Three pairs of yellow and white lovebirds had perched on the side of a fire engine. A colourful flash across the darkness revealed an Amazonian parrot circling just outside the light of the flames.

'At least he seems to have given his livestock a fighting chance,' Fyfe said.

'Among them the Phyllobates terribilis he claimed was impossible to breed in our neck of the woods.'

'A little yellow lie but how were we to know?'

'What do you suppose he's done with the frogs?'

'Emptied them out of their tank.'

'Then they could be anywhere.'

'What were we told? They either fry in there, or freeze out here.'

'Either way that's the end of it.'

'Who knows?'

Something exploded inside the fiercely burning building and there was the crash of falling debris. A shower of orange sparks rose into the air. The firemen with breathing apparatus reappeared at the door, hurrying away from the building. One removed his helmet and mouthpiece and spoke to a senior officer who was writing on a pad. From that distance Harper and Fyfe couldn't hear what he said but they saw him shake his head. The ambulance closed its doors and set off down the bumpy track.

'Nobody inside, Connor. It's not the end yet.'

'Oh fuck.'

'And if Guthrie's done a runner he might have taken his favourite pets with him rather than let them loose here.'

'Frogs you mean?'

'The killer frogs. Did you notice that Guthrie's van has gone.'

'You're right. I missed that.'

Harper thought deeply, remembering the start of the first video; the moon seen through the tree branches, panning downwards. Virginia's favourite place and Guthrie's favourite pets.

'I bet I know where he's gone,' Harper said.

'You lost the first bet.'

'The law of averages dictates better odds on this one being right then.'

'That's what detective work is all about.'

'Worth a shot, isn't it?'

'Could be another wild goose chase but lead the way,' Fyfe said. It had got much colder suddenly. 'Looks like the fire is going out here anyway.'

The cemetery gates were still sealed by the blue and white incident tape warning people to keep out. Fyfe ducked below it. Harper followed him. They knew what they were going to find because Guthrie's van with its broken brakelight and tied-on bumper was parked haphazardly on the verge.

Inside the circular wall everything had been beaten flat during the mandatory fingertip search for evidence relevant to Virginia Stevenson's untimely death. Nothing had been found. The gravestones seemed more numerous with the undergrowth removed: and to be standing at even crazier angles than Fyfe remembered. He counted the days since he had come through the gates to be witness to the first of several deaths. It had been Monday morning, now it was Thursday night. Four days. Such a short space of time. When his first grandchild was born what factor would those days be multiplied by to give her her lifespan?

It was cold inside the cemetery walls and silent. In the murky evening light no bird sang, no animal moved. Even the wind had died down, leaving the tree branches overhead perfectly motionless. Guthrie was sitting by Virginia's grave, leaning against the fallen statue of the angel. Harper's torch beam picked him out and the two policemen walked over to him. His grey-haired head was bowed and he was wearing the apron he had had on when they visited him. One hand was in the apron pocket, the other was stretched out and lay cupped, fingers pointing upwards as if they were growing out of the ground. It was right beside the eye of the stone angel, which seemed to be peering into it and studying it curiously. They both crouched down. Harper took hold of Guthrie's hair and gently pulled back his head to be able to see his face. His eyes were half closed and his mouth gaped. A trickle of spittle had dried on his chin. There were strange red spots on his cheeks like a clown's make-up. He was very obviously dead.

'His hand,' Fyfe whispered. 'Look at his hand.'

In Guthrie's hand was the mangled remains of a small yellow frog. The body was crushed but the head was relatively undamaged. Its black eyes stared out and its mouth was still grinning obscenely.

'Don't touch anything.'

'Don't worry,' Harper said. 'Looks like he took the same way out as he imposed on the others. There must be more poison than blood in him if he took a mouthful of his pet frog.'

'Must have been some hallucination he rode out on,' Fyfe said. 'An apocalypse all to himself inside his head.'

'The Nightmare Syndrome, our toxicologist called it. Whatever it was, it put an intolerable strain on his heart. He'd no need to jump out of a window.'

'It's all over now. We'd better call the scene of crime boys in to go through the proper procedures here.'

'That's it then.' Harper stood up and shone the torch around randomly. 'We have motive, cause and effect but no real reason for all this.'

'Keep a sense of proportion, Connor. Finding the ultimate meaning of the great mystery of life and death is not part of our job description.'

'Just as well.'

'We would never make it stand up in court.'

'Old man Guthrie might have given us a few pointers from his Bible.'

'It didn't seem to help him much.'

'All is vanity he said, remember. So it doesn't matter.'

'That's all right then.'

'You're right,' Harper conceded. 'There's nothing more to be done.'

'Not for Guthrie. We can take a back seat. Let's you and me delegate responsibility and go home to spend some time with our loved ones. We can catch up soon enough tomorrow.'

'Sounds good to me.'

Fyfe caught sight of the weathered inscription on the statue plinth behind Guthrie's head. It was suddenly illuminated by the moving torch beam. Somebody had been scraping at it, tracing the individual carved letters to make it more legible. It was easy to read, even in the brief instant before the darkness swallowed it again. Until The Day Breaks.

He looked up. The tree branches were swaying slightly, smearing their blackness across the grey sky. There was no moon. Daybreak was a long way off.

46

Thursday: 23.22

Connor Harper sat on the floor of his bedroom and drank whisky straight from the bottle. Kelly lay in the bed. She had the sheets rumpled up at her throat, her head on the pillow, and a petulant expression on her lovely face. She had been annoyed when he rang the bell to get in because he had forgotten his keys in his haste to get away earlier in the evening. At one point, after Fyfe had dropped him off in the street and headed home, he began to suspect that she had left his flat again in a huff, to punish him for abandoning her. Then she was back with him, complaining into the intercom before she would operate the automatic catch and flouncing away as soon as he got inside the door of the flat. He didn't fight with her. She grumbled that he had woken her in the middle of a fantastic dream and now she wouldn't be able to return to it. Despite her grumbling she was fast asleep within five minutes.

Harper got the whisky, watched the blue movies for a while, and then went to the bedroom to sit and watch Kelly. He examined her face in minute detail, noticing new things about her like the shape of her hairline high above her forehead, and the pattern of creases on her lips, and wrinkles on her eyelids. Her twitching eyes indicated that she was dreaming once more, perhaps back in the swing of the dream he had interrupted, safe and secure within the boundaries of her own fantasy world. He tried to imagine what was going on inside her head. Kelly stirred, made little mewing kitten-like noises and snuggled down contentedly into the pillow. It certainly didn't seem to be the Nightmare Syndrome, as described by Professor McDougall. Her floppy bunny slippers were under the bed, their eyes hidden under their big ears.

The strength of the spirit made his eyes water but it had the effect of calming him, making his wandering thoughts seem less urgent and his own existence less important. He had promised Fyfe he wouldn't drink but the temptation was too great now that he was on his own. There was only half a bottle left in the house anyway so he couldn't get absolutely wrecked. He would make it to work in the morning and Fyfe would never know. He could earn his living, provide for his family, and plan his next holiday. How lucky could a man get?

This was as good as it got, he thought bitterly. A successfully completed case, underlings ordered to do his bidding at a ridiculous hour of the night, and a beautiful girl in his bed. If his life stretched out into the future like this he would have no complaint. If only part of the deal was that he didn't have to grow any older.

Harper tried to think what Sarah Smith might be doing. The skinny girl he had found in the filthy squat would be somewhere in the city, lying in somebody's bed, probably tripping happily on some combination of street-bought drugs that would soon kill her. Again he had this crazy, recurring idea that he would go out and find her, rescue her from her cruel destiny, save her from herself. In different circumstances, different times, they might have met, clicked, and started to live together as lovers. It was not so far-fetched. It could so easily have been Sarah in his bed rather than Kelly. Every time he was out on the streets from now on he would be searching for Sarah, looking over his shoulder, watching out for her face in the crowd. He might find her before she ended up on a mortuary slab, he might not. So many things were ruled by sheer chance.

161

Kelly shifted again, turning right over to face the other way and pulling the covers with her so that Harper could only see her hair spread across the pillow. She needed some privacy for her dreaming apparently. He pursed his lips and blew across the top of the bottle to make a hollow, echoing sound. The harder he blew the louder the sound. By varying it he could make a tune of sorts. It amused him for a long time, until the bottle was empty. Eventually he climbed into the bed beside Kelly and put his arm over her and allowed himself to drift off to sleep into what would hopefully turn out to be the most pleasant of nightmares.

47

Thursday: 23.55

David Fyfe lied. He didn't go home as he had said he would. Instead he drove straight to the main police headquarters on the edge of the city centre and flashed his identity card at an officer he didn't recognize behind the reception desk. He punched the security code number into the pad at the secondary door, getting it wrong twice before it finally clicked open. From the outside the building looked empty and deserted with most of the light concentrated around the entrance area, as if it had been drained from the rest of the building to pool there. Hypostasis it was called in dead bodies; the blood, no longer being circulated, began to obey the laws of gravity instead. He remembered as a fresh-faced rookie being called to a scene where a victim had lain for two days at a steep angle on a flight of stairs. Violence was suspected because the face was all purply black with what looked like severe bruising. The pathologist laughed. It was the blood, Roger Somerville had explained, filling the skull and soaking into the skin. Cause of death was later established as a simple heart attack. Case closed.

Fyfe went straight to the main incident room. Few people were around. Most of the nightshift were back at the cemetery. Matthewson, dozing with his head on his arm, was in his usual place and there were others who vanished round corners ahead of him or side-stepped into rooms as he approached. The place was nearly empty, giving the impression of a great ship abandoned in the moment before she went belly up. Fyfe curled his right hand into a loose fist and dug his fingernails into the palm to check he was not hallucinating. No. It was all real enough.

'Have you got a Bible, Bill?' he asked.

Matthewson looked up blearily. 'Not on me,' he said.

'You know the verse about everything being vanity.'

'Vanity of vanity, saith the preacher. All is vanity.'

'Exactly.'

'One generation passeth away and another generation cometh, but the earth abideth for ever.'

'How true. Did I tell you, Bill, that I am going to be a grand-father?'

'Congratulations, sir.'

'Another generation on its way.'

'Yes, sir. I put your messages on your desk.'

Matthewson dropped his head back onto his arm and Fyfe went over to his small office partitioned off at the side of the room. He was, as always, surprised to see that it looked exactly the same despite everything that had happened since he had left it. He closed the door behind him to protect himself from the emptiness and slumped down in his chair so hard that it moved backwards and bumped against the thin wall, making it bulge alarmingly. He began to look through the messages but he was very tired. The one on top of the pile was from Somerville, saying that everything had gone smoothly and there was no need to worry. Every now and then opaque grey blots slid across Fyfe's eyes, blurring his vision. Mostly they went down, but occasionally they disobeyed the laws of gravity and travelled upwards. Fyfe took this as a good sign that hypostasis had not yet set in on him.

Guthrie had looked peaceful in the graveyard, smug even. Fyfe knew the same poison would be found in his blood as had killed the others. There was a certain self-contained completeness to the episode. His brood of killer frogs would be out there some-where, shivering in the cold of an alien climate as their blood

163

congealed inside them. Hungry foxes or cats or crows would be their only victims now, otherwise the danger would evaporate and nature would claim them for its recycling programme. Fyfe would become a grandfather and life would continue. Except Fyfe didn't believe it was all over. No fat ladies had yet sung. It wouldn't be as neat and tidy as that. It never was.

Mental exhaustion caused his thoughts to run into each other. With faces swirling confusingly in the background, the dead Guthrie kept being replaced by his mad but very much alive son-in-law who would turn into Kate's new man who would in his turn become the dead Bruce Davidson suddenly lunging at him. The threatening image came into sharp focus as an eye blot slid clear, dropping away like a tear. It made Fyfe jerk away instinctively and hit the wall again.

He took a deep breath and put his feet up on the desk. At least Kate was safe from Doug's violent mood swings. He would be detained overnight and another doctor would sign the section form in the morning to extend it to two weeks. By then, they would have him under control. He dumped all the other message slips in the waste bin except one. It was a request to contact a London number and was marked urgent. There was no name and Fyfe did not recognize the number. But for some reason he was troubled by it. He closed his eyes, put his head back, and tried to think who it might be.

He visualized himself back in his sitting room at home but this time the sofas were occupied by the dead girls Virginia and Belinda. Connor Harper was with them, sharing a bottle. Guthrie too. And Sally and Kate discussing babies. Fyfe looked up and saw that in the corner was the stone angel. It toppled over as he watched, its shadow falling on top of him first, then its full weight. Fyfe twitched and the chair moved. He woke up and for a second wondered who the person was floating in the darkness directly in front of him, with the city street lights and shadows shining right through him, before becoming aware that it was just his own reflection in the window.

Fyfe thought about going home but since it wasn't yet midnight he decided to dial the London number to satisfy his curiosity. It rang for a while before it was answered. At first there was a lot of crackling and white noise as though the receiver had been dropped. Then the line stilled and settled. Fyfe didn't say anything.

'Hello? Hello? Who's there?'

The accent was thick with sleep but nonetheless immediately familiar. The friendly stranger in the pub who had helped him carry out the violent assault on Doug who was now confined to his very own padded cell or whatever was the modern psychiatric equivalent. This was it then, the loose end that ruined the perfect symmetry of events. The stranger must have somehow found out who he was, probably from the hotel, maybe from another source. There were too many blank periods in that night which Fyfe just didn't remember when the opportunity must have arisen. The stranger hadn't helped out of the goodness of his heart and concern for a drinking pal. There was an ulterior motive. Fyfe, staring into his own reflected eyes, was almost glad.

'Hello? Who is this? Do you know what time it is?'

Fyfe decided that he would bluff. He cleared his throat and announced himself, enunciating carefully. 'This is Detective Chief Inspector David Fyfe.'

'Is it now,' the stranger replied after a brief hesitation. 'At this time too. And do you know who this is?'

'I haven't the faintest idea.'

'You should have. We met recently. Don't you remember?'

He could have been sitting opposite Fyfe so clear was the sound of his voice. They could have been back in the pub, face to face, drunkenly agreeing that there were times when natural justice demanded extraordinary action. He could smell the leather bomber jacket, see the bent nose and the small scars round his eyes and the blue tattoo of the spider's web on his neck. Even as they shook hands and the chairs scraped back and they went to get the sawn-off scaffolding poles for the premeditated attack, Fyfe had been wondering vaguely what was in it for the stranger. Now he knew.

'I don't believe I remember anything,' Fyfe said.

'I think you do.'

'No. I'm afraid not. You must be mistaken.'

'No mistake. I know what you did, Chief Inspector, and I am sure your superiors would be interested to learn about your behaviour.'

'You must have the wrong person.'

'You are the right person and you know it. I could make life very difficult for you.'

Fyfe thought calmly about his options. He could pay up or he could brazen it out, deny everything and express astonishment that he should be accused of such a thing. If he chose the first course, there was the clear risk that the stranger would then keep coming back for more. The second was favourite then. In police investigation terms there was nothing to link him with the stranger. A few witnesses from the pub perhaps, easily discredited. He had personally disposed of the mask he had been supplied with and any forensic evidence in the house was useless because he had been there before. There might be fingerprints on the scaffolding pole but he could claim it was a set-up. Forensic evidence in the car was circumstantial and a half-competent defence agent could make it look as if it was planted. Doug, a paranoid schizophrenic recently committed to a madhouse, was a fairly unreliable witness. No court would convict Fyfe on evidence like that. It needed a confession to make the allegations stick.

'My life is difficult enough already,' Fyfe said.

'I warn you, Chief Inspector, I'm not bluffing. I will expose you if you don't admit what happened.'

There was a hint of frustration creeping into the stranger's manner. He was realizing that he was not in control of the situation as he had expected. If they had not been 400 miles apart he would have resorted to violence and had Fyfe by the throat.

'Are you blackmailing me?'

'I'm asking you if you value your good name and career.'

'Not really.'

'Policemen can't ignore the law just because it suits them.'

'Why not?'

'Because . . . because it isn't right.'

'I don't care.'

'I think you do.'

'Then you don't know me very well.'

An uneasy silence indicated to Fyfe that the stranger was beginning to have doubts. He would see the same inadequacies in his allegations, the lack of proof. What he wouldn't appreciate was that Fyfe's reputation might be enhanced rather than damaged if somebody accused him of defending the honour of his pregnant daughter in such a practical manner. It was the only way others would learn what he had done.

'It would be better for you if you admitted it,' the stranger said.

'I never admit to anything.'

'You can admit it to me.'

'No I can't.'

'Yes you can. I know who you are and where you are.'

'Are you sure you're not hallucinating?'

'Absolutely certain. I can come and get you any time I want.'

'I'll look forward to it.'

'I don't want to make this hard for you.'

'Then piss off and die.'

Fyfe slammed the phone down. The stranger would now back off or try again. It was an evens bet either way. In many ways it was good to have uncertainties ahead. It made life interesting, made the heart beat quicker.

He knew now was the time to return to the bosom of his family, to his wife, and to his dogs, and to his daughter and her latest fancy man and to his quietly developing embryonic grandchild, harbinger of the next generation. But he also knew he wasn't going to go back to that warm, inviting bed. He needed to stay away, keep his distance. He felt the restlessness running like a benign poison through his veins.

Still with his feet on the desk he reached for the phone again and dialled Hilary's number from memory. It rang for a long time before being answered. Again there were more indistinct scrabbling sounds followed by the sound of deep breathing and a silence. He imagined Hilary lying in her bedroom, sprawled face down across the big bed where he had left her less than twenty-four hours before, lying like the fallen angel in the cemetery. The curve of her backside and shoulders would be reflected in the wall of mirror doors with the phone to her ear as she waited to hear who it was.

'Want to go swimming?' he asked.

The silence crackled before a gruff male voice answered: 'Who the fuck is this?'

Fyfe reacted slowly but before another word was exchanged he had put the phone down and sat back in his seat. 'Nobody,' he said to himself. 'Nobody at all.'

He stared at his likeness hovering in the night beyond the glass of the office window. The blots descended over his eyes. It was like diving underwater, blurring and distorting the confusion of images competing for attention inside his head. When his eyes cleared he could see that he was smiling broadly. Who would have predicted such an outcome to the day, he thought? And now it was after midnight. Another day. Life was still interesting. Still uncertain. Time to go home.